STEELE RIDGE CHRISTMAS CAPER BOX SET 1

A STEELE RIDGE HOLIDAY ANTHOLOGY

TRACEY DEVLYN   KELSEY BROWNING

ADRIENNE GIORDANO

STEELE RIDGE
www.SteeleRidgeSeries.com

Edited by Martha Trachtenberg

Cover Design by Elizabeth Mackey

Tracey's Author Photo by Lisa Kaman Kenning, Mezzaluna Photography

Kelsey's Author Photo by Trashy Betty Photography

Adrienne's Author Photo by Debora Giordano

Digital Edition, September 2020, ISBN: 978-1-948075-67-1

Print Edition, July 2021, ISBN: 978-1-948075-73-2

STEELE RIDGE CHARACTERS

The Steeles

Griffin "Grif" Steele - Steele sibling. Sports agent and Steele Ridge's city manager. *(Going HARD)*

Carlie Beth Parrish - Blacksmith and love interest of Grif Steele.

Reid Steele - Steele sibling. Former Green Beret and head of Steele Ridge Training Academy. *(Living FAST)*

Brynne Whitfield - Owner of La Belle Style boutique and love interest of Reid Steele.

Britt Steele - Eldest Steele sibling. Construction worker who has a passion for the environment and head of Steele-Shepherd Wildlife Research Center. *(Loving DEEP)*

Miranda "Randi" Shepherd - Owner of Blues, Brews and Books, aka Triple B, and love interest of Britt Steele.

Mikayla "Micki" Steele - Steele sibling and Jonah's twin. Master hacker who returns home after a decade of self-imposed exile. *(Breaking FREE)*

Gage Barber - Injured Green Beret and Reid Steele's close friend who comes to Steele Ridge to help run the training center and love interest of Micki Steele.

Evelyn "Evie" Steele - Youngest Steele sibling. A nurse who travels around Western North Carolina, providing medical care to those in need. *(Roaming WILD)*

Derek "Deke" Conrad - Commander of SONR (Special Operations for Natural Resources) group and love interest of Evie Steele.

Jonah Steele - Steele sibling and Micki's twin. Video game mogul and former owner of the billion-dollar gaming company, Steele Trap. Responsible for saving the town of Steele Ridge, formerly known as Canyon Ridge. *(Stripping BARE)*

Tessa Martin - Former in-house psychologist at Steele Trap and love interest of Jonah Steele.

Joan "Miss Joan" Steele - Mother of the six Steele siblings, guiding light of the family, and Eddy Steele's wife. *(Enduring LOVE)*

Eddy Steele - Father of the six Steele siblings and Joan Steele's husband.

The Kingstons

Margaret "Maggie" Kingston - Eldest Kingston sibling. County Sheriff whose office is based in Steele Ridge. *(Craving HEAT)*

Jayson "Jay" Tucker - Pro football player and love interest of Maggie Kingston.

Kristofferson "Cash" Kingston - Kingston sibling. Firefighter and tactical medic. *(Tasting FIRE)*

Emmy McKay - ER doctor and love interest of Cash Kingston.

Wynette "Riley" Kingston - Youngest Kingston sibling. Ethnobotanist and family brainiac. *(Searing NEED)*

Coen Monroe - Delta Force operator and love interest of Riley Kingston.

Harris "Shep" Kingston - Kingston sibling. Adventure guide who navigates life with Aspberger's with his trusty canine companion Puck. *(Striking EDGE)*

Jocelyn "Joss" Wynter - Rock star and love interest of Shep Kingston.

West "Way" Kingston - Kingston sibling. Gunsmith expert and former recon Marine. *(Burning ACHE)*

Roni Fenwick - Former FBI agent and CIA trainer. Love interest of Way Kingston.

Ross Kingston - Father of five Kingston siblings and stay-at-home dad, rock of the family, husband of Sandy Kingston, and CEO of Kingston Farm and Market.

Sandy Kingston - Mother of five Kingston siblings, Miss Joan's younger sister, wife of Ross Kingston, former environmental engineer, and a foodie-in-training (aka purveyor of inedible food).

THE MOST WONDERFUL GIFT OF ALL

STEELE RIDGE CHRISTMAS CAPER #1

TRACEY DEVLYN

1

———

THE THROATY *TEAKETTLE TEAKETTLE TEAKETTLE* OF A Carolina wren pulled Randi Shepherd from a deep sleep. Bright light filtered through her eyelids, indicating she'd slept much later than she should.

Today was a big day. She and several of the Steele and Kingston ladies were meeting at Blues, Brews, and Books this morning to assemble several dozen holiday-themed raffle baskets.

Last week, multiple wildfires had ravaged parts of Western North Carolina, leaving behind a swath of charred debris and homeless Carolinians. Along the northern border of Steele Ridge, the fires destroyed a multigenerational apple orchard, a tree nursery, and a small subdivision before moving on.

The families and businesses had lost everything —their homes, their possessions, their pets, their livelihoods, and their presents.

Heartbroken by their misfortune, Randi decided to organize a benefit to solicit donations of food, clothing, toys, furniture, and much-needed funds. The town's residents responded exactly as she'd hoped, with enthusiasm and generosity.

Prying one eye open, she glanced at the bedside

clock and groaned. It was worse than she thought. If she didn't drag her bottom out of bed now, she'd be late.

She threw back the covers and the cool cabin air prickled her bare skin.

"Where do you think you're going?" A strong arm curled around her waist, dragging her back into a warm haven of male temptation. Britt Steele's muscled leg slid between hers, drawing her closer, flesh to warm flesh. He nuzzled the side of her neck and kissed the outer shell of her ear.

"I have something I want to share with you."

Anticipation rippled down her spine, not stopping until it tingled her toes. Lifting her head, she peered at the one man who could make words dry up on her lips with nothing but a sexy glance in her direction. "You're in a *very* sharing mood this morning."

"A man can never"—he flexed his hips—"share too much with the woman he loves."

She reached back and raked her nails over his bare leg. "A genuine open book, aren't you?"

"To some." His warm, calloused hand skimmed down her side "To you."

"I don't have time to play this morning. The girls will be at Triple B within the hour."

"The event isn't until this evening."

When his big body half-covered hers, she experienced a familiar, delicious vulnerability. It was always so with him. He made their every encounter erotic and intense and new.

In all other areas of her life, she took charge, made decisions, kept things moving. But with Britt, in moments like this, she *succumbed*. Without thought, without fear, without regret.

He drew her hand from where it clutched his leg and placed it on the rumpled sheets in front of her. "Hold on."

Her nails dug into the fabric, anchoring her for the oncoming storm. "We're prepping this morning." The ladies had volunteered to give up their Saturday to help her prepare for the benefit tonight. She couldn't leave them standing outside Triple B while she indulged in another bout of fun with her mountain man.

"Me too," he murmured, nuzzling her shoulder.

"I'm serious."

"Sounds like I'll have to skip a few preliminary steps." His voice was thick with need and promise. "And get right to the good part."

Breathing became irrelevant. All her aching body needed was *him*. Needed him to feed the desperate hunger that writhed inside her, that begged him to put words into action.

Blood rushed, breaths heaved, skin brushed against skin. Sensation after sensation arrowed through her every nerve ending.

Then she splintered. Shattered into a million brilliant pieces of stardust. Britt soon followed, his exhausted body slumping against her.

After.

The after-minute, when their breathing swayed together and their heated bodies melded into one harmonious being, was the moment she yearned for at odd times during the day. It was these sixty seconds when she felt wholly connected to another human being.

Loved. Protected. The one place where she belonged without condition or expectation.

It was pure joy.

As soon as the aftershocks subsided and her body ceased its trembling, Britt brushed his lips over her shoulder. A sweet ache spread through her muscles. Missing him already.

Stretching, she snaked a hand around the back of his neck, guiding him to her mouth for a long, luxurious kiss.

His hand skimmed over her ribcage before cupping the underside of her breast. And just like that, one touch from this man awakened her satiated body.

As always, their bodies spoke their own language, expressed their physical needs in nothing more than movement. He came over her, surrounded her in a cocoon of flesh and bone and home.

God, she loved the feel of him, the scent of him —she tangled her tongue with his—the taste of him.

"If we keep this up," he whispered, "you won't make it to your prep fest."

Her eyes flared open to check the clock on the bedside table and she moaned at the amount of time that had slipped by. "I have to go." Her tongue flicked against his upper lip. "To be continued."

Peeling away from her, he sat back on his haunches and stared down at her exposed naked body with the hunger of a man who hadn't experienced release in months, rather than minutes.

"Do you ache," he pressed a curled knuckle between her legs, "here?"

A sharp breath hissed between her teeth, and she considered plunging into round two with him.

Groaning, she sat up, kissed the center of his chest, and left their warm bed.

He eased onto his back like a sultan sprawling against a mound of silken pillows. Knee raised. One arm braced behind his head, the other one resting on the rumpled sheets near his hip. Pure enticement.

She turned away before she changed her mind and stretched her arms over her head, enjoying the slow release of knots in her back and shoulders. Anxious energy began to flow through her veins as her mind picked through all the tasks that needed to be accomplished before nightfall.

"Your lower back could use a good stretching," Britt coaxed. "Maybe you should touch your toes."

She glanced over her bare shoulder to find his attention riveted on her bottom. "You know, I think you're right."

With the smoothness of a Cirque du Soleil performer, she bent forward until her fingertips grazed the wooden floor.

An animalistic growl preceded the savage flinging back of sheets.

A shriek escaped her throat before she bolted into the bathroom. She twisted the lock in place a whisper before he reached the door. Heart pounding, she stared at the golden oak stained panels waiting, anticipating . . .

A delicious roar of defeat thumped against the barrier, then silence settled in on the other side. Her pulse tripled its pace.

"Miranda."

She closed her eyes. "Go away, Britt. I have to get ready."

"After, then."

His promise sent a surge of heat between her legs. She reached for the door handle, wanting nothing more than to feel the burn of his mouth on her body. Every. Single. Inch.

Then the echo of Evie Steele's sweet but commanding voice speared through the sensual fog enveloping her good sense.

Don't let my brother keep you in bed all morning. We have a lot of baskets to assemble.

Randi smiled and kissed the door at the precise location where she knew his forehead would be resting. "After."

2

"ONCE YOU FINISH PASSING THESE OUT," RANDI handed off a stack of colorful flyers to Aubrey Steele before zipping up her teal fleece jacket, "come back inside and work your bow-tying magic on the finished baskets."

The daughter of Grif Steele and Carlie Beth Parrish, sixteen-year-old Aubrey, with her mischievous smile and strawberry blond hair, was already breaking young male hearts.

"Okay." Aubrey took the flyers and pivoted toward an approaching trio of older teenage boys. "Hey, Jon, Roger, Hunter. Will you share this with your parents? We're collecting donations to help the people affected by the wildfires."

Roger kept walking, Hunter skimmed the flyer's contents, and Jon appeared captivated by Aubrey.

Most girls her age would spend equal time checking their reflection in Blues, Brews, and Books's large picture window and thumbing through their social media feed. But not the daughter of Steele Ridge's blacksmith and city manager. Like her parents, Aubrey tackled every project with focus and gusto.

A crisp December breeze buffeted Randi's cheeks and stray snowflakes tumbled along its current. White holiday lights glinted in the parkway trees and Glenn Marks jingled his Salvation Army bell outside Brynne's clothing boutique, La Belle Style.

Even though signs of the approaching holiday surrounded her, Randi struggled to find her Christmas spirit amidst so much profound loss and heartache in and around her community. If she couldn't embrace the joy of the holiday, what must those who'd watched their homes burn to the ground be feeling?

"Jon, Hunt," the sullen, disinterested Roger called from several shops away, "come on."

"Will you be at the benefit?" Jon asked Aubrey.

She nodded. "I'm on raffle ticket duty."

Hunter folded the flyer and shoved it into his back pocket. His square jaw sported a full five o'clock shadow any adult male would envy and his dark eyes probed too deeply for one so young.

Given the pink tint piling into Aubrey's cheeks, Randi wasn't the only one affected by the boy's stare. But for completely different reasons.

Hunter whapped the other boy's shoulder with the back of his hand. "Let's go."

"Save me a ticket," Jon said.

Aubrey smiled. "How about two?" Her gaze darted toward Hunter before refocusing on Jon.

The latter returned her smile. But it wasn't smitten Jon who held her attention as the two strode away.

"Careful with that one," Randi warned.

"We're just friends," Aubrey protested. "Well, sort of. He's in my English class."

"I'm not talking about Jon."

"Neither am I."

Randi opened her mouth to deliver more advice she didn't have any business giving, but Aubrey rushed to stick a flyer in front of a passing preteen girl, who held the hand of a thumb-gnawing little boy.

"Give that to your parents—" Aubrey took in the girl's features, her eyes flared in recognition, and then all the color in her cheeks disappeared. "Oh, I'm so sorry."

The preteen averted her gaze, toward the interior of Triple B. After several seconds of awkward silence, she asked, "How are you going to get all those baskets to the wildlife center?"

"My uncle Britt and cousin Cash are going to load them into their trucks and haul them over."

"Do you need any help putting the baskets together?" A hopeful note entered the girl's voice and her green eyes stopped short of pleading.

Aubrey glanced at Randi.

"Thank you, sweetheart," Randi jabbed her thumb toward her helpers inside, "but we have a well-oiled assembly line going on in there right now. If we add another set of hands, it could blow the whole thing apart."

The girl's shoulders sagged a bit. She nodded and strode off, tugging the boy behind her.

Hugging the flyers to her chest, Aubrey groaned into her hands. "I'm such an idiot."

"What was all of that about?"

"I told her to give the flyer to her parents."

"Yeah, so?"

"Her dad was killed in a vehicle accident not long ago."

"How awful."

Aubrey buried her face in her hands. *"Idiot, idiot, idiot."*

Randi pulled her hands away. "It's a mistake that any of us could've made."

"Doesn't make me feel any better."

Wrapping an arm around the girl's narrow shoulders, Randi said, "Try to focus on the good work we're doing for the families instead, okay?"

"Mom's bummed that she couldn't be here."

"We miss her, too, but the project she's working on could very well take her blacksmithing career to a whole new level."

A proud smile split through the sadness etched on Aubrey's sweet features. "She's afraid she won't make her delivery date, but I know she will."

Randi brushed a hand over the girl's strawberry blond waves. "She always does. I'm going back in to make sure the ladies are behaving."

"Prepare for disappointment."

"I'm going to tell them you said that."

Aubrey flashed an unapologetic smile.

When Randi reentered the restaurant, gratitude filled her chest.

An organized line of Steele and Kingston women were assembling dozens of raffle baskets, their bulging contents compliments of the town's generous residents.

Riley Kingston, on one of her rare visits home, unpacked the donated items, Evie Steele organized them into themes, and Brynne Steele arranged them in the baskets. Joan Steele logged each basket's contents, Micki Steele took a photograph of the arrangement, and Sandy Kingston wrapped the whole bundle in cellophane and held it together at the top with a sturdy rubber band. Tessa Martin lined each one up on the bar, where they awaited Aubrey's bow-tying skill, and Kris McKay kept all of the stations clipping along.

"That's it," Riley said, breaking down the last cardboard box.

"Perfect timing." Kris stood back and eyed their masterpieces. "The restaurant opens for lunch in an hour."

Evie's face fell. "This was so much fun. I don't want it to be over yet."

"You might be on to something," Miss Joan said. "We should get the Steele and Kingston women together more often to do charitable work."

"What a great idea," Brynne said. "Hopefully, Carlie Beth and Maggie can join us next time."

"It would be good for Maggie to be around women more," Sandy said. "Between supervising a bunch of mostly male police officers and entertaining Jayson's football teammates, it's a wonder she hasn't grown testicles."

"Mama!" Riley scolded—or tried to around a bubble of shocked laughter.

"Well, it's true."

"What's true?" Aubrey asked, joining them, eyes twinkling.

Joan's lips twitched. "Never you mind, young lady." She pointed to the line of baskets on the bar. "Get to work."

Aubrey huffed. "I'm old enough to hear Uncle Reid talk about jock itch, but not old enough to discuss testicles?"

Miss Joan looked to Randi and the other ladies for guidance, but they all ducked their heads to hide their smiles. Since no help would be forthcoming,

Joan responded in her no-nonsense grandmother's voice, "Not today."

"Oh, no," Sandy exclaimed.

"What's wrong?" Riley asked.

"I brought fudge squares for us to share." She dug her keys out of her purse and held them out to her daughter. "Would you be a sweetheart and go get them?"

Riley shared a glance with her cousin, Micki, before accepting the keys. "Of course."

"What kind of fudge, Aunt Sandy?" Humor danced along the corners of Micki's eyes, though she kept her tone nonchalant.

Everyone else held their breath.

"Grape and kale with a white chocolate twist."

Female glances of horror zipped across the room.

Good Lord, Randi thought. One day Sandy Kingston would combine two opposing ingredients that would either cure cancer or put them all in a coma for a week.

3

BRITT PULLED DOWN THE ALLEY, TOWING A COVERED trailer full of donated clothes, toiletries, and furniture for the folks affected by the wildfires. His cousin, Cash, hauled a similar load. Once they added the gift baskets to the back of their trucks, they would take everything over to the wildlife center for distribution.

"What a cluster," his best friend Deke Conrad said, peering into the side-view mirror. "Cash didn't make it through the opening you created."

Reaching the back of Triple B, Britt drew Old Blue to a stop. "He probably got flagged down by someone." The paramedic knew everyone.

"No wonder Grif recommended moving the benefit to the wildlife center. Between the craft fair and road construction, logistics would've been a nightmare."

Britt opened his door. "Let's secure the tarp to the bed before we load the baskets."

Unlocking the covered trailer, Britt located the blue vinyl tarp and tossed several bungee cords to Deke.

Thunk. Thunk. Thunk.

Turning his attention to the rhythmic sound overhead, Britt found a young boy on a third story balcony, with headphones on and his back against the apartment building's rusted railing. He bounced a ball in the small space between his legs and the brick wall with a listlessness that suggested he'd been at it for a while. And was bored out of his skull.

At that age, Britt would've lost his mind if he'd been forced to find entertainment on a four-by-three balcony. Especially now that the earlier snowflakes had given way to a sunny, wind-free day.

Kids needed to be active and their minds challenged. Not for the first time, the idea of hiring a naturalist to develop more children's programs crossed his mind. He had funding sitting in an account, but he hadn't been able to spare the bandwidth to post the job and go through the interview process.

The bulk of his time and attention had been focused on establishing Steele-Shepherd Wildlife Research Center as North Carolina's premier research facility for endangered red wolves. A goal he could now proudly say he'd achieved.

The only drawback to his success was that the center's educational component was nonexistent. He spared another glance toward the boy. A failing he would remedy soon. Today's explorers were tomorrow's naturalists and future supporters.

He knew the perfect person. Deke's coworker, Keone Akana, spent a lot of his own time visiting local schools and educating the kids on the importance of bats, bees, butterflies, and other pollinators. Maybe he'd be interested in a part-time paying gig. He made a mental note to give Akana a call.

Britt strode to the rear of his truck and shook out

the tarp, throwing one end to Deke. The vinyl crackled as they fanned the protective rectangle over the empty bed. Once they reached the front of the bed, they hooked bungee cords into the grommets at each corner and let them hang against Old Blue until they could tie all four corners down.

An engine roared behind them.

"There's Cash," Deke said.

Britt nodded at the tarp. "Let's roll this back."

Thunk. Thunk. Thunk.

The boy continued his solemn play, tweaking loose a long-ago memory of when an eight-year-old Jonah broke his hand in gym class and couldn't play video games for several weeks. Instead, he'd spent days watching recorded episodes of *Teenage Mutant Ninja Turtles,* with Reid joining in whenever he could, until Britt dragged his ass outside to play a game of one-handed basketball.

Once they finished preparing the bed, Deke said, "I'll check in with the ladies and see if any of the baskets are ready for loading."

"Ask Randi if she has time to throw a couple of burgers on the grill. I'm starving."

"Is the second burger for me or you?"

"Depends on how many baskets you load."

"I predict enough to warrant some fries, too."

"Don't get cocky." Britt nodded in the direction of his cousin and Coen Monroe. "Better add a few more for those bozos as well."

Deke smirked and headed into the well of estrogen.

Thunk. Thunk. Thunk.

Britt stalked over to the emergency stairwell and slammed his palm against the metal railing several times.

Whipping around, the boy stared down at him.

Britt motioned for him to remove his earbuds.

Popping them out of his ears, the boy leaned closer until his forehead rested against two rust-flaked spindles.

"You want to make five bucks?" Britt asked.

"Doing what?"

"Carrying baskets."

The kid's eyes narrowed in suspicion. "I don't see any baskets."

"They're still inside Triple B." Britt hooked a thumb in the direction of the restaurant. "We need some help loading them into our trucks."

"Five dollars?"

Britt dug into his front pocket, separated a bill from the others, and held it out. "Deal?"

The boy climbed to his feet and made his way down the metal stairs and over to Britt. He accepted the fiver. "Deal."

Britt gave the boy's boney shoulder a reassuring squeeze in the same way his father had done to him three decades ago. "What's your name?"

"Marc."

"Hello, Marc. I'm Britt." With the flick of his chin, he indicated the two newcomers. "Let's go meet the others." He led him over to where the guys leaned against his truck.

"Who do we have here?" Cash asked.

"Marc, this is my cousin Cash and our friend Coen."

The two men shook the boy's small hand.

"Marc is going to help us load the trucks."

"Good," Cash said. "We need someone to pick up Coen's slack."

"The only slack on my part is not insisting on driving over here."

"In case you hadn't heard, I'm a paramedic. I can maneuver a rig through anything."

"You almost ran over the same dog twice."

"He darted out in front of me."

One of Coen's brows flared high. "Twice."

"It happens."

Marc's attention zigzagged between the two men, unsure.

Coen noticed and held out his fist to the boy. "Partners?"

Marc responded to the fist bump, a guarded smile appearing.

Thirty minutes later, Britt followed Marc, carrying out the last of the baskets. "This should be number forty-eight."

"Sixty-one in Cash's truck," Deke said. "Bringing our total to one hundred and nine."

"The good people of Steele Ridge really came through for Randi," Cash said.

"It's a good cause," Britt said. "A crisis every one of us might face someday."

"What cause?" Marc asked, climbing onto the back wheel of Old Blue.

"We're collecting items for the families who lost their homes a few months ago."

"Lost their homes?"

"Careful sport." Coen walked by and scooped him off the wheel. "You won't like it if Cash has to stitch up your noggin."

"Do you remember the wildfires that blew through not long ago?" Deke asked, drawing the tarp over the bed and tying it down. Britt followed suit on his side.

Marc nodded.

"One of them destroyed several homes and a few businesses."

The boy dropped his gaze and turned quiet.

"Marc," a young female voice called from the apartment balcony above. "What are you doing?" A brown-haired girl peered down at them with suspicion.

"Helping."

"Time to come in. Lunch is ready."

"I'm not hungry."

"It won't keep." She made a hard gesture with her hand for him to join her. "Come eat."

"I—"

Britt put a hand on Marc's shoulder. "We're done here. Don't let your food spoil."

Anger carved a deep V in the boy's forehead before he stomped toward the staircase.

"You were a big help today," Britt said.

"See you around, kiddo," Cash said.

"Bye, Marc," Deke said.

Coen stood silent, watching his small partner ascend the staircase until he disappeared into the apartment.

Randi stuck her head out Triple B's back door. "You boys ready to eat?" She shot Britt a meaningful glance. "Maybe food will improve your mood."

"There's nothing wrong with my mood."

"As sweet as a fuzzy baby bear." Deke made a hacking sound and spat on the ground.

Coen raised a brow.

"A loogie of bullshit," Cash interpreted.

At the open door, Britt shot the assholes behind him a one-finger salute.

Laughter followed him inside.

4

"WHAT'S WRONG?" RANDI ASKED BRITT TWO HOURS later as they stood in the wildlife research center's parking lot.

He stared into the back of Old Blue. Rather than answer, he barked out a command to Cash.

"Count your baskets."

"I already did. There's sixty-one."

"Count them again."

Something in Britt's tone kicked Cash into action. His cousin unfastened the tarp, ripped it back, and did a quick tally. "Fifty-six."

"Five are missing here too," Britt said in a hard voice.

"Missing?" Randi asked. "Where could they have gone?"

"The trucks were left unattended for a good half hour while we ate. Anyone could have swiped them."

"What a shame," Randi said. "The families could have used the money we would have raised from raffling the baskets."

"Help me unload my truck," Britt said.

Randi stilled. "What are you going to do?"

"Go find them."

"Whoever took the baskets is long gone," Coen said.

"Someone might have seen something."

"What about organizing all of the donated items?" Randi asked.

"I won't be long."

"There's no way I can talk you out of this, can I?"

The bullheaded man continued offloading baskets with singular focus.

"I'm going with you, then," she said.

"Who's going to organize things here?"

"We'll take care of it," Deke said.

"The ladies will be arriving soon to help set up," Coen added.

Britt eyed all of them before nodding. "Let's go."

They both jumped into Old Blue, saying little during the drive back to town. Once they rolled into the alley, Randi said, "I hate the thought that someone from our community could be so uncaring."

He parked a good distance away from the back of Triple B. "Why do you assume they're uncaring?"

"Because they stole from people who are in need."

"It's possible their need was greater."

Sadness gripped her chest. "I hadn't thought of that."

He brushed a stray tendril away from her face. "Or they were thieving opportunists." He nodded down the alley. "Let's see if our thieves left any evidence behind."

After exiting the truck, they walked the length of

the alley. Randi had been down this alley a thousand times, but today little things stood out in a way they never had before. The cracked window in Mrs. Hannaby's kitchen, the grease-stained rags hanging over the stair railing behind Hank's Hardware, and the tiny, abandoned bird's nest tucked in the corner of a concrete ledge and downspout.

"What are we looking for?" she asked.

"Anything out of the ordinary."

"Isn't an alley where everything out of the ordinary goes to hide?"

"Good point. Just call out anything that might be tied to our caper."

She found nothing but the obligatory cardboard box, stray beer bottle, lipstick-stained cigarette butt, and abandoned trash bags. All of which appeared to have been there for more than a few hours.

Once they reached the back of Triple B, she asked, "What now?"

He glanced around before lifting his attention to the empty balcony three stories up.

Following his gaze, she asked, "What's cooking in that brain of yours?"

"Maybe Marc or his sister saw something."

"You want to question the kids?"

"Seems like a logical next step." Sensing her hesitation, he asked, "You don't think so?"

"You gave Marc a positive experience. Asking him questions about a theft could leave him with the opposite."

"I'll make my intentions clear."

Dread filled her stomach.

Britt moved to stand in front of her, cupping her cheeks in his hands. "Trust me?"

She brushed a lock of shaggy blond hair away from the corner of his eye. Her big, gruff mountain man had a heart as big as the sun and a smile, when he chose to share it, that could light up the darkest room. "With my life."

He kissed her forehead. "Then let's go see what we can find out."

After making their way to the front of the building, they ascended three flights of stairs. No matter Britt's reassurances, Randi couldn't squelch her unease. Every step closer to Marc intensified the sensation.

The apartment building was clean but well-worn. The hallway carpet looked like it should have been replaced a decade ago and a cold draft wrapped around their ankles.

"This should be it." Britt rapped his knuckles on door 306.

"Who is it?" a young female voice asked.

"Britt Steele. I'm here to see Marc."

"Why?"

"He helped us load some things earlier. I need to ask him a few questions."

"About what?" A note of hesitancy entered the girl's voice.

"Would you please let us speak to Marc or go get your parents?"

"Us?"

"Miranda Shepherd is with me."

A rustling behind the door followed a muffled argument.

"Is everything okay?" Randi asked, leaning closer.

"Yes," the girl gritted out.

"Something's not right." Britt tried the door-knob. Locked.

More rustling.

He rattled the knob again.

"Maybe I should call the police," Randi said.

"Let go of me!"

"Marc?" Britt asked.

Something collided with the door.

Randi pulled out her phone. "Knock it down, Britt."

A second before his boot slammed into the door, it was wrenched open by a panting Marc.

Sprawled on the floor behind him was a girl, maybe eleven or twelve, with a scratch on her chin. Recognition niggled at the back of Randi's mind, but she couldn't come up with a name.

A much smaller child propped in the corner of the couch burst into tears. The girl scrambled to her feet and ran to him, cradling him in her arms and murmuring soothing words in his ear. When he began to quiet, he started gnawing on his thumb.

The girl handed off the little boy to Marc and positioned herself between the boys and the adults. "You need to leave."

"What's your name?" Randi asked.

"None of your business." She pointed to the open door. "Go."

"Jayla. Her name is Jayla."

"Marc!"

He gently pulled the younger boy's thumb from his mouth. "This is Aiden."

"What are you doing?" Jayla asked, breathless.

"Britt's not going to hurt us."

"You don't know—"

"He was *nice* to me."

Jayla stared at her brother for several seconds before relenting. Without looking in their direction, she bit out, "Ask your questions."

"Did you see anyone around our trucks after we loaded the baskets?" Britt asked.

Everything in the apartment stilled, even Aiden. Rather than answer, Marc kept his attention on his sister.

"Why? What happened?" Jayla asked.

Britt didn't bite. He crossed his arms and hiked up one brow.

"Some of the baskets your brother helped load have gone missing," Randi said when silence grew too thick for her comfort.

Britt slanted her an irritated look.

"Someone stole them?" Jayla asked.

"Yes," Britt said.

Jayla crossed her arms in a perfect imitation of Britt's stance. "Maybe they blew out of the back of your truck."

"They were covered by a tarp."

"Maybe it came loose. "

"You're offering a lot of maybes." Britt began to stalk around the room. Jayla didn't take her eyes off of him.

"Did you see anyone?" Randi asked.

"We were eating. Same as you."

"So you didn't observe anyone by our trucks?" Britt pressed.

"Didn't I say so?"

"No, you're dancing all around it."

"We saw the food on our plates."

"When do your parents come home?" Randi asked.

Marc interjected, "Our mom—"

"They don't need to know our business," Jayla interrupted her brother.

"Where is your mom?" Britt asked, directing his question to the boy.

Marc glanced at his sister, who sent him an almost imperceptible shake of her head. "At work."

"What does she do?" Britt asked.

"We've answered your questions about the theft," Jayla said. "I need to put Aiden down for a nap."

"You haven't—"

Randi curled her hand around Britt's elbow, silencing him. "Thank you. If you hear anything about the baskets, please come see me at Triple B."

"You work there?" Jayla asked.

"She owns the place," Britt said.

"I'm there most days. If I'm away, Kris McKay will know how to contact me."

"You're going through a lot of trouble for a few baskets," Jayla said.

"We were going to raffle them off and give the money to the families who lost their homes and livelihoods to the wildfires."

The girl's attention shifted to her brothers before she whispered, "I hope you find them then."

Randi smiled. "Feel free to stop by my place any time. We have a nice assortment of books in our Little Free Library." She guided Britt to the door. "Your first cookie is on me."

Once they reached the alley again, Britt glanced up at the empty balcony. "They know something."

"Yes, but we can't strong-arm them into telling us. We toed a very thin line by speaking to them without their parents present." She pulled out her keys and unlocked the back door of Triple B. "What was all that about, anyway?"

"What do you mean?"

"All of that alpha posturing. You're normally so gentle with kids, especially girls."

He blew out a frustrated breath. "She reminded me of Micki at that age. Always trying to bullshit her way out of a corner."

She stroked the back of one finger over his cheek. Sometimes she forgot about how, at a very young age, he had to become a father figure to his siblings. The weight of all that responsibility must have been unbearable, at times.

Grasping his hand, she led the way to her office. Once inside, Britt settled into his favorite rocker-recliner and Randi sagged onto her well-worn pleather sofa, propping her feet up on the coffee table.

"They might be protecting an older brother," he said.

"Why do you say that?"

"A family photograph on one of the end tables. He appeared to be three or four years older than Jayla."

In the depths of her memory, puzzle pieces finally clicked together.

"Aubrey knows the family." At Britt's look of surprise, she explained. "Your niece and I exchanged a few words with Jayla earlier."

"Why?"

"We handed her a benefit flyer. After the exchange, Aubrey mentioned that the kids' father had been killed in a vehicle accident not long ago."

"Damn. That explains a lot."

"What do you mean?"

"Despite the shabbiness of the building, the kids' clothing, the furniture, and the knickknacks all appeared to be of good quality."

"You think they relocated after their father died?"

"It's possible. Did Aubrey say anything else about the family?"

"Not that I recall."

"Where's Aubrey?"

"More questioning?"

He nodded.

Randi shot off a text. Her phone pinged seconds later. "She's at home."

He pushed to his feet. "Let's take a ride."

"Are you sure it's a good idea to involve Aubrey?"

"All we're doing is finding out what she knows, if anything, about this family."

"You're right." She rubbed the space between her eyebrows. "There's something about this situation that's so unsettling."

He brushed his lips over hers, deepening the kiss when her tongue slid along the inside of his upper lip. They both released a long breath as if their bodies had been anticipating this moment for hours.

Randi slipped her hands beneath his shirt and jacket, needing to touch his warmth, flesh against flesh. She would never tire of exploring every plane, every ridge, every inch of this man.

Her lips journeyed from his mouth to his chin, his jaw, and the hollow at the base of his throat. She forced his shirt up, revealing a cut stomach and an unfathomably broad chest.

She leaned in to run the top of her tongue over one too-tempting nipple.

A low, agonized groan rumbled up from his throat. In the back of her mind, she knew this was neither the time nor the place. Silverware clinked in the distance and the clomp of a dozen busy feet sounded outside her office. The restaurant was still in full lunch mode.

With the scent of Britt in her nose, the feel of him beneath her fingers, and the taste of him in her mouth, she couldn't bring herself to care.

It was a good thing Kris McKay pushed into the office when she did or her assistant manager would've seen a lot more of her boss that she cared to witness.

"Oh, crap," Kris mumbled, backing out of the room. "Sorry!"

Randi stepped away from what would've been a delicious after-lunch dessert. "It's okay, Kris. Did you need something?"

"Nothing that can't wait five"—her dark eyes roamed over Britt's unmoving form—"fifteen minutes." She slammed the door shut.

Randi smiled. "I finally managed to shock her."

Britt reached for her, and she backed away, holding out a hand to stop him. "Save it for later, big guy."

"We have fifteen minutes." His features turned molten. "I can take care of us in seven—with the right inducement." He stepped toward her, and Randi put a table between them.

"Aubrey, remember?"

The mention of his niece poured the right amount of cold water on his ardor. His chest rose, then fell. "Later."

Rather than the aching, needful quality of this morning when he'd spoken to her through the bathroom door, the single word held not a promise, but a command.

Her body shuddered as anticipation curled around every tingling nerve ending.

"Later."

5

RANDI SHIFTED FROM ONE FOOT TO THE OTHER AS Britt knocked on the blacksmith's door. She still didn't feel quite right asking Aubrey questions, but neither of them could come up with a better alternative.

A muffled female voice answered, "It's open."

Britt stuck his head inside. "Can we bug you for a second?"

Carlie Beth looked up from what she was working on and pushed her protective goggles to the top of her head. "Please do. You'll be saving me from the brink of insanity."

He opened the door wider, and Randi strolled into one of the most interesting workspaces in all of Steele Ridge. Carlie Beth's forge didn't look like much from the outside. The gray metal building hid an array of machinery and tools that created works of art when manipulated by the right set of hands and guided by one of the most talented minds in the region.

"Not going well?" she asked.

Dressed in denim coveralls, a navy top, and heavy leather apron, Carlie Beth set down a large metal object on a nearby table and shed her gloves. She gave Randi a welcoming, but weary, smile. "Oh, you know the life of an artist. Nothing's ever quite perfect." She wiped her hands on an already-grimy hand towel. "Did you get everything delivered to the center?"

Randi nodded. "Aubrey did a great job with the basket bows."

"She came back bubbling with stories." Carlie Beth winced. "I'm so sorry I couldn't join you."

"Don't apologize. This project could put your business on the radar of some well-connected, influential people."

"Thank you. If only Aubrey had an interest in blacksmithing, I could get some free labor out of the deal."

"I have a feeling Aubrey's time wouldn't come cheap," Randi said.

"Speaking of Aubrey," Britt said, "is she around?"

Carlie Beth cocked her head to the side. "She's inside trying on dresses for the benefit. Do you need to speak with her?"

He nodded. "We wanted to ask her a few questions about a girl she knows, and her family, if that's okay with you."

"Is something wrong?"

"Some of the food baskets were stolen from our trucks."

"That's terrible."

"We have a suspicion of who it might be and thought Aubrey could shed some light on the kid."

"Let me go grab her."

A few minutes later Carlie Beth returned with a disheveled Aubrey in tow.

Britt strode over to his niece and gave her a big hug. "Sorry to pull you away from your primping."

"Did someone really steal our baskets?"

"A few," he said. "We need to ask you about a boy you might know."

"What's his name?"

"We're hoping you can tell us."

"Do you know where he lives?"

"In the apartment building behind Triple B."

Randi added, "We think he might be related to the young girl and little boy you spoke to outside Triple B this morning."

"Jayla Robbins?"

"Does she have an older brother?"

Aubrey nodded. "Damon. But he's not who you're looking for."

"Why not?" Britt asked.

"Because he's dead."

"Dead?" Randi asked, unable to keep the shock from her voice. "How?"

Aubrey dropped her gaze to the turquoise ring on her middle finger. "He died in the same car crash as his dad."

Carlie Beth wrapped an arm around her daughter. "Did you know him well? I don't recall you ever mentioning his name."

"Not really. We were lab partners in biology last year."

"Do you know how the accident happened?" Britt asked.

"About four months ago, Damon was practicing driving with his dad and he collided with a semi."

Randi glanced at Britt, confusion marking her brow. "If Jayla's brother is dead, who was she protecting?"

"Good question." Turning back to Aubrey, he asked, "Do you know anything about the mother?"

Aubrey shook her head. "Sorry."

Randi smiled. "No worries, sweetheart. You did great."

Britt leaned over and kissed his niece on the forehead. "Thank you. Now go select your prettiest dress. I want to watch your dad squirm when all the boys flirt with you tonight."

Aubrey sent her uncle a conspiratorial look. "You're my new favorite uncle."

6

THE TINY BELL HANGING OVER THE DOOR JINGLED, signaling a customer had entered the café side of Triple B.

"Good morning," Kris said to the newcomer. "I haven't seen y'all in a long time."

Straightening from her bent position over the small refrigerator, Randi glanced behind her to find Jayla and her two little brothers standing on the opposite side of the coffee bar's counter. "Good morning." She twisted the plastic cap off the soy milk jug. "Are you here for your cookies?"

Balancing Aiden on her hip, Jayla gave her a tentative nod.

Marc rose up on tiptoes to inspect the array of sweets displayed behind the protective glass. "They have brownies."

"Brownies!" The youngest Robbins bounced in his sister's arms.

"How about you, Jayla?"

She pointed to a tower of cookies. "Oatmeal and raisin, please."

"Kris," Randi said, "why don't you take them

over to the reading area and see if they can each find a book."

"You got it."

Although Randi had made the offer for the kids to stop by, she never imagined that the defiant girl would take her up on her offer. But she was glad Jayla had. Notwithstanding the kids' tragic loss, something about the trio called to Randi's protective instincts.

Pulling out a serving tray, she arranged three plates in a triangle, then placed a sweet on each. Next, she added utensils, napkins, a glass of soy milk, a glass of orange juice, and a glass of water, not knowing what the kids would enjoy. She picked up the tray and started around the counter, when a small container of cut fruit caught her eye.

Ripping off the lid, she squeezed the container into the circle created by the plates. Randi stared at the crowded tray, wondering if she'd gone overboard. One look at the kids lined up on the reading couch, with wide smiles on their faces and books in their laps, and her uncertainty disappeared.

Randi slid the tray onto the low table before the couch. "I hope you're hungry."

Jayla took in the bounty. "You said a cookie." A hint of excitement mixed with suspicion curled around her words.

"I'm feeling generous this morning. It's a beautiful sunny day, and I have three new friends." When the trio didn't move, Randi asked, "Is something wrong?"

Jayla glanced at her brothers, the food, Randi, and then back at her brothers before giving the boys a sharp nod. The two wasted no time tearing into their brownies. The little one leaned forward and dug a grape out of the container and popped it in his mouth.

Randi asked the youngest, "You like grapes?

Aiden nodded.

She pulled a chair close and sat across from her mysterious visitors. "What are the three of you up to today?"

Jayla shrugged. "Nothing much."

"Are you getting excited about Christmas?" Kris asked.

Aiden nodded, vigorously.

"What did you ask Santa for this year?"

"A big truck."

"That's it? Just a big truck?"

"And Mama."

Randi and Kris shared a frown, noticing the other two siblings stilled. "Why would you need to ask Santa Claus for your mama?"

"Because—"

"Aiden, eat your brownie," Jayla demanded. When the girl's attention shifted to Randi, she tried for a smile, but failed. "Mama's under the weather right now. He just wants her to feel better."

A sick feeling started low in Randi's stomach and spread into her limbs. She rose. "Well, y'all enjoy your food and books. Feel free to stay as long as you like. If you need anything else, let me know."

On unsteady legs, Randi strode away, not stopping until she reached her office. After closing the door, she braced a hand on a filing cabinet and bowed her head, concentrating on breathing.

In out. In out. In out.

She wasn't sure how long she stood there battling a sense of dread, a battle that she could not win. But sometime later, a hesitant knock sounded behind her.

Plastering an easy smile on her face, she opened the door. Jayla stood in the hallway, peering into Randi's office, an uncertain expression in place of her normally defiant one.

"How did you—?"

"Kris showed me the way," Jayla blurted out. "You said if there was anything else that I needed to come find you." The girl twisted her fingers together. "Did you mean it?"

"I don't make false promises. Come inside and tell me what's on your mind."

Jayla sat on the edge of the sofa, her right knee pumping up and down like an oil rig on speed. Taking her own seat, Randi did her best to look relaxed, and waited.

"Thank you for the food," Jayla began, "and the books. My brother, Marc, loves to read."

"Does he spend hours at the library?"

"No, it's too far for him to walk alone."

"He's welcome to use my library, any time."

The girl's features softened in gratitude.

"How can I help you, Jayla?"

"I wondered—if you had—I mean—"

"Take a deep breath," Randi suggested.

Jayla inhaled a deep breath, her narrow chest lifting. "Do you have any small jobs around Triple B that you need help with?"

Randi didn't know what she'd expected the girl to request, but it wasn't a job.

"There're always odd jobs to do. There's never any lack of work and too few hands to help."

The girl's face brightened. "I'm a really hard worker. I'll do whatever you need."

The dread she'd been battling engulfed her chest.

"You would have to get permission from your mother, Jayla. I could get in trouble, otherwise."

"Mom won't mind."

"That may be—"

"Please," Jayla whispered.

Randi leaned forward and placed her hand over the girl's bouncing knee. "Are you in trouble?"

The girl's breathing increased. "I would just like to help my family. My brother and father"—she swallowed hard—"are gone. It's been . . . difficult. I want to help."

What she had deemed as defiance in the girl was in fact bravery and strength and resourcefulness. And terror.

It took several seconds for Randi's words to work their way around the tightness in her throat. "How long is your school break?"

"A couple of weeks."

"Report to me here tomorrow, at eight o'clock."

The girl jumped up, and Randi caught the glitter of tears in her eyes.

"Thank y-you," Jayla said.

"Feel free to bring your brothers. They can read while you work."

"You won't regret it." Jayla ran from the room.

"I know I won't," Randi whispered.

7

BRITT SPOTTED HIS COUSIN, SHERIFF MAGGIE Kingston, cruising down Main Street and signaled for her to pull over.

Sprinting across the road, he waited for her to roll down the window. "Busy?"

"I'm on my way to see Grif," she said.

"Mind if we ride and talk?"

"Hop in."

Once he settled into the passenger seat and the vehicle was on its way, she asked, "What's up?"

"I have an odd request."

"After the last few years, odd no longer applies to our two families."

"No one can argue that fact."

"Before we get into your question," Maggie said, "how are the benefit preparations going?"

"They were going pretty well until some of the gift baskets disappeared."

"Stolen or misplaced?"

"Stolen."

"How many?"

"Enough to irritate the hell out of me."

"Is that why you flagged me down?"

"Yes and no."

"You've got five minutes before we reach our destination."

Britt filled her in on the thefts and their interview with Robbins kids.

"You spoke to the kids without an adult present?"

He gave his cousin a sideways glance. "I already heard it from Randi."

"What do you need from me?"

"Whatever information you can get for me on the Robbins family."

"What do you hope to uncover?"

"I'm not sure."

Something in the Robbins apartment had felt vaguely familiar to Britt. He couldn't quite put his finger on the connection, but he would.

Maggie pulled into a parking lot and he noticed his brother, Grif, decked out in an expensive black leather coat and gray dress slacks, standing with two other suits. "Big meeting?"

"You know Grif, always wheeling and dealing."

"Thanks for the help, Maggie. I owe you one."

"You owe me a dozen," she pushed open her door and made to exit, "but who's counting?"

He gave her ponytail a sharp tweak before jumping out of her vehicle. Retribution sizzled in her brown eyes as she glared at him over the squad's hood.

"Am I interrupting something?" Grif asked, joining them.

"Only your brother's death."

"In that case, maybe I should come back in five minutes."

"Prick."

Grif grinned. "What brings you here? A burning interest in capital investments?"

Sometimes it amazed him that he and Grif had come out of the same womb.

"Just spending some quality time with my favorite cousin."

Maggie snorted.

"I'll let you get back to business." Britt turned back toward town.

"You're going to walk?" Grif asked.

"It's only a couple of miles."

Grif dug into his pocket and held out his keys. "Take mine, and I'll hitch a ride back with Maggie."

Britt saw the emblem on the key fob and glanced around the parking lot, confirming his suspicion. "Um, no thanks."

Grif lowered his hand. "It's a minivan, not a pink Cadillac."

"I'd rather drive the Caddy."

"One day, you and Randi will have a few rug rats running around, and you'll appreciate my choice of transportation."

Britt shook his head. "I have three letters for you, bro. S-U-V." Shoving his hands into his front pockets, he strode away.

"Hey," Grif called.

"I'm not taking your damn minivan."

"Mom mentioned some of the Blackwells would be at the pre-event prep dinner."

Maggie moaned.

Every year, his Kingston cousins held a holiday festival at their farm. Family members who helped out with the event were treated to an amazing dinner beforehand. Aunt Sandy and Uncle Ross used the time to address any last-minute issues and to make sure the event's themed costumes fit properly.

They liked to try different things to draw folks in. This year, they had decided to invite Bigfoot. North Carolina's craze for the elusive hairy creature had finally spilled over into the festival. Britt had even constructed a photo stand-in board, featuring the big guy.

Bigfoot joining the party bothered him far less than the Blackwells.

"We need to put together a battle plan," Grif said.

Britt glanced between his brother and his waiting business associates. "You coming to the benefit?"

"Yep."

"You?" he asked Maggie.

"Yes."

"Let's talk then."

Britt resumed his trek back to town, his mind no longer on gift baskets and thieves and strong-willed girls. His thoughts shifted to much more dangerous territory.

Blackwells.

There'd been a few attempts to bring his Black-well cousins more into the fold, over the years. Most had either failed or had met with a lukewarm reception. Somehow Maggie had established a professional relationship with Ash—or Cameron—Cam —or whatever the hell name he used at the FBI —Blackwell.

No telling how long it would last. The whole Blackwell clan was nothing but a giant question mark. Never more so now that they'd renovated an old church camp into a fortified quasi-military compound.

Or so he'd heard from the rumor mill. Only a select few people were allowed beyond the entrance gate, and those folks kept a tight lip about the goings-on of their employer.

Smart. No telling what his cousins would do to loose-lipped employees.

His mom and Aunt Sandy must be over the moon about this new development. He wondered what had enticed the Blackwells to the dinner—Bigfoot or his aunt's Tofu Turkey?

Britt shook his head to dislodge the Blackwells from his thoughts and refocus on the Robbins mystery. He wished like hell he could figure out what was nagging him about their apartment.

He hoped whatever it was didn't lead to a dark secret.

8

RANDI HEARD THE FAMILIAR TREAD OF HER ASSISTANT manager nearing her office. "Kris?"

Kris craned her head inside. "Need something?"

"Do you have a second?"

"Sure." She closed the door behind her. "What's up?"

"The Robbins kids." She leaned back in her desk chair. "You seemed familiar with them."

"They come into the café every Sunday with their mother."

"When did you last see them?"

"I don't know. Maybe three weeks ago."

"Any idea why they haven't been in?"

"None." Kris plopped into the rocker-recliner. "Why the interest?"

"After the theft, Britt and I visited Marc to ask if he saw anyone suspicious hanging around the trucks."

"Did he?"

"His sister jumped in before he could say much."

"She's always been protective of her little brothers."

"We left their apartment with the sense that something wasn't quite right."

"What do you mean?"

"Before we learned about the horrible vehicle accident, we thought she might be covering for her older brother." She shrugged. "Now, I'm clueless."

"No leads on the basket thefts, then?"

Randi shook her head. "I'm certain Jayla is hiding something, though."

"Everyone is hiding something."

Randi thought back to the time when she and Britt were battling each other for the rights to her family's property. Both had harbored secrets, not the least of which was their growing attraction to each other.

"What did Jayla want with you?"

"A job."

"Job?" Kris's eyebrows rose high into her forehead. "How old is she, ten? Eleven? Twelve?"

"I'm guessing the latter."

Kris studied Randi. "You agreed."

"It's contingent upon us not breaking any child labor laws."

"What would lead a twelve-year-old to apply for a position in a bar?"

"You make it sound as though Triple B is some sleazy bug-infested dive."

"You know what I meant. What would force a girl her age into employment? Do you think she's getting pressure from her mom?"

"Maybe. She said something about things being tight after her dad died." Randi shrugged. "Either way, we could use a few extra hands around here."

Kris rose and wrapped her arms around Randi. "You are the best, you know that?"

Heat burned her ears. "It takes little effort to say yes."

Kris drew back, giving Randi a knowing smile. "It's more than that, and you know it."

"Don't you have work to do?"

Kris laughed. "Yes ma'am."

Once she was alone again, Randi sat back in her chair, extending her legs out in front of her and crossing them at the ankles. She steepled her fingers in front of her face and replayed Kris's question in her mind, over and over.

What would force a girl her age into employment? What would force a girl her age into employment?

When the answer came to her, a stinging sensation formed at the backs of her eyes. She refused to let the tears fall. She had to be strong, she had to be smart.

Like Jayla.

9

"Eat it," Jayla demanded.

"No."

She stared down at her brother, her fear growing like an fire bubbling in the pit of a volcano. Some nights, she woke gasping on the toxic fumes. Certain she wouldn't—they wouldn't—survive.

"Marc, I don't have time for this. I need to get to work."

"It's not right."

"Whath's not righth?" Aiden asked, chewing on his thumb.

"Finish your ramen soup." Jayla drew his hand away from his mouth. "We're leaving in ten minutes."

"To the Tipple Bee?"

Despite the pressure of the clock ticking away, she smiled and brushed a hand over his blond hair. It was getting too long. She would have to cut it soon.

"Yes, the Triple B."

"I want s'ghetti," Aiden whined, in a perfect imitation of his older brother.

"But what we have is soup. Eat."

Her attention shifted to Marc, her sensitive brother. Not even for him would she allow her family to starve.

"Not eating your soup won't make things right, Marc. Don't waste it."

Sending her a glare, he picked up his fork and stabbed at the slippery noodles. She didn't turn away until after he'd eaten five mouthfuls. Then she shifted her hard stare to Aiden until he did the same.

She hated being a jerk, but if that's what it took to get her brothers to eat soup for breakfast, then that's what she'd do.

"When you're done, go get dressed," she said.

After grabbing her clothes out of their shared bedroom, she slipped into the bathroom and finished getting ready for the day.

Fifteen minutes later, she emerged, bracing herself for another fight. To her relief, her brothers were milling around by the front door, coats on, and superhero book bags hooked over their shoulders.

She picked up their abandoned bowls and walked them into the kitchen. When she caught a whiff of the chicken-flavored broth, her stomach growled. Aiden had left a little bit of broth in the bottom of his bowl and she tipped it up to her mouth. Her body screamed for more. But there was none, at least not for this meal. She had to make the food last as long as she possibly could.

She had to be strong.

She had to fight.

Right and wrong no longer existed in her world.

Only survival.

10

BRITT STOOD NAKED IN HIS BEDROOM, USING THE thick towel to scrub the water out of his hair.

After leaving Maggie, he'd come back to the cabin to get ready for the benefit. Given the events that had unfolded today, the special "after" event he'd hoped for would have to wait. He'd had everything planned, down to the candles he would light. The scenario ran through his mind's eye, each detail vivid and precious. His palms began to sweat.

Later. When the time was right.

He stared into his closet, wondering what the hell he should wear. Socializing wasn't his thing, but Randi would never forgive him if he didn't go.

It wasn't that he didn't believe in the charity, he just hated small talk. No, not hated it. He wasn't good at it.

Shaking his head, he went back into the bathroom and let the hot water run for a full minute before cupping his hand underneath the stream. He splashed the steaming water on his face and picked up his razor. With efficient strokes, he removed the stubble from his cheeks and chin and neck.

Setting aside his mixed feelings about tonight,

his mind wandered back to the small, third-story apartment. What would it be like to lose your father and big brother in a split second? How would a twelve-year-old react when she suddenly found herself as the eldest sibling? Would she adapt and take on the leadership role? Or would her anxiety get the best of her?

When his father had slowly disappeared from their lives, Britt had gone through a series of emotions over months, years. Confusion, denial, anxiety, anger. It took a while for his Steele determination to kick in. Every day, he waited for his dad to return. Every day, he waited for some ancient wisdom to rise within him and tell him what to do. Every day, he'd been disappointed.

It wasn't until he heard his mom sobbing in her room that the bone-deep acceptance that his dad would not return had slammed into him. From that day forward, he became the man of the house. He'd taken care of his siblings the best way he knew how.

Britt's hand lowered as an awful realization took hold, one that would explain the weird vibe he'd detected while in the Robbins apartment.

His phone rattled against the porcelain sink, startling him.

Maggie.

He tapped the razor hard against the rim three times and set it aside before swiping his thumb across the screen. "What'd you get?"

"The vehicle accident you were asking about?"

"Yeah, did you find something?"

"It's not good."

"Go on."

"The report states that sixteen-year-old Damon Robbins was driving a silver Lexus LX on Highway

276 when his vehicle collided with a semi. Damon was declared DOA and they transported his father to the hospital, where he died two days later."

He winced. "Damon was driving?"

"On his driver's permit."

"In a Lexus LX? That's a big vehicle for an inexperienced driver, especially on a busy mountain road."

"There's more."

"I'm listening."

"One of my dispatchers lives in the same apartment building as the Robbins family."

"What's her impression?"

"Solid middle-class family." "About a year ago, Mr. Robbins got laid off from his job at the hospital as a radiologic technician. To save on expenses, they moved into the two-bedroom apartment back in June."

"Their troubles started well before the accident."

"Would seem so."

"Anything else?"

"According to Lindsay, my dispatcher, Mrs. Robbins has been seen less and less over the last few months. And not at all in the last week."

A dark foreboding sank deep into the pit of his stomach. "Where does she work?

"She arranges flowers at Ava's."

Located downtown, the popular florist shop had been around for as long as Britt could remember. The owner, Ava Russo, must be pushing eighty, by now. Maybe he would stop in there on his way—

"Before you get any ideas, I've already spoken to Ava. Mrs. Robbins hasn't been to work in over a week."

He closed his eyes a moment as the painful confirmation of what he'd feared hit him. "She's gone."

"Which means the kids might be all alone." Sharp edges scored Maggie's words. "I'm on my way to the apartment to verify."

"If it's true, what are you going to do?"

"Alert child and family services."

"What about contacting other family members?"

"My staff is already working on it."

"What happens if you don't find the mother and you strike out with other family?"

A long silence blared through the phone. "Then the kids will go into the system."

Britt braced a hand on the sink and stared at the remnants of his beard dotting the porcelain bowl. Once the kids were in the system, their chances of staying together would be zip.

Jayla's defiant features and her battle stance made sense now. She knew, even at her young age, that if adults found out about their situation, she would lose her family. And like any head of the household she was going to fight to the death to prevent that from happening.

Even if it meant stealing charity baskets.

11

TAKING THE STAIRS TWO AT A TIME, RANDI AND BRITT cleared the third-floor landing and rushed down the hallway to where a deputy stood guard outside the Robbins apartment.

Deputy Leia Lou turned to face them as they approached.

"May we go in?" Randi asked.

Leia shook her head. "Sheriff gave me strict orders that no one is to enter."

"We've been working with Maggie on this. Can you please check in with her?"

"Wait here."

As soon as Leia entered the apartment, Randi and Britt crowded into the open doorway. The scene inside broke apart her heart.

Little Aiden sat in the corner of the couch chewing on his thumb, tears sliding down his cherub face. Marc stood at the balcony door, with a bulging backpack secured to his shoulders. A smaller, superhero pack hung from his fingers.

Jayla stood toe-to-toe with Maggie, arguing.

"This is kidnapping," Jayla said.

"No one is kidnapping you," Maggie said. "We're

taking you someplace safe until we can locate your mother."

"You don't need to locate her. She's not lost."

"Tell me how I can contact her then."

"She dropped her cell phone in the toilet a couple of days ago and hasn't had a chance to get a new phone."

"Give me an address. I'll send a deputy."

"If you send a deputy, she'll get fired."

"What time do you expect her home?"

Jayla glanced at the clock on the wall. Several seconds went by before she said, "She's normally home by 5:30, but I think she had some errands to run first."

Unflappable Maggie showed her first sign of irritation. "It seems your mother's having a bad day."

Officer Lou took the opportunity to step forward and whisper in the sheriff's ear. Maggie glanced up at them, her expression flattened into a look of resignation before responding.

When Leia rejoined them, she said, "Sheriff said you can go in, but don't interfere."

Randi nodded and stepped through the portal with Britt at her heels.

As they approached, Jayla's eyes widened. "What are you doing here?"

"To offer some support."

"Support for who?"

Randi froze, not knowing how to answer. She didn't want to see the kids taken into child protective custody. But she also didn't want them living here alone. If Jayla had been a handful of years older, the situation might not seem so dire. But a twelve-year-old could not—should not—be forced to care for her younger brothers.

"All we want is for you and your brothers to be safe."

"We're safe *here*," Jayla said, with the first hint of desperation leaking into her words.

"For now," Britt said. "What happens when word gets out that there are three unprotected kids alone in this apartment?"

Uncertainty skittered across Jayla's face, and Randi knew the girl hadn't considered that situation. She'd probably worked through a hundred other scenarios, but not that one.

Jayla blinked and her familiar determination settled in place. "We're not alone. Our mother will be home soon, and she'll give you a blistering for the way you're treating us."

Aiden's soft whimpers broke through the small protective barrier he'd try to erect between himself and the loud adults. He emitted a sorrowful wail that had Jayla jerking around and scooping him up into her arms.

The boy clutched his big sister while shudders racked his small frame.

"Do you have any other family we can contact, Jayla?" Randi asked.

Jayla shook her head.

Randi tilted her head in Britt's direction, not sure what else to ask, but instinctively knowing he would understand.

A large hand smoothed up her back and settled in the crook of her neck and shoulders. The simple gesture made her want to press her body into his side and absorb all of his strength. But Jayla stood before them, alone, rock solid, with no one to comfort her.

Randi braced her feet apart and squared her shoulders.

"How about a compromise?" Britt suggested.

"What do you have in mind?" Maggie asked.

"Randi and I will camp out here until Mrs. Robbins comes home."

"What if she doesn't come home?"

"Then it's your call."

Maggie's sharp gaze scanned the room in one thorough sweep. Randi could see the sheriff wasn't pleased with the offer, but wasn't herself ready to hand the kids over to child protective services.

"If I don't hear from you before," Maggie said, "my deputies will be here first thing in the morning to collect the kids."

"You okay with that, Jayla?" Britt asked.

The girl's expression reminded Randi of a hunted animal, pausing at a crossroads. When one direction led to a hungry wolf and the other to a ninety-foot cliff.

Before she could answer, Deputy Lou released a long, slow whistle.

"What?" Maggie demanded.

She held up a large basket wrapped in cellophane. "Does this look familiar?"

Randi strode to where the deputy stood beside the couch and peered into the small space between the couch and the wall. Nine baskets full of food, toiletries, and gift cards lined the tight space. Aubrey's purple bows adorned the outside of each one.

Closing her eyes, she swallowed back the ache in the back of her throat before turning to address Jayla.

"Why?"

A line of moisture trembled in Jayla's eyes, but she remained quiet.

"So we could eat," Marc said into the tension-filled silence.

He didn't turn to face the room, just continued to stare out the window. The calm resignation in his voice made him sound twenty years older.

"Where's your mom, Jayla?" Britt asked.

Finally, Marc turned. "She won't answer you."

"Will you?" Maggie asked.

His attention settled on his older sister, the two of them having a visual battle of wills. A few seconds later, he nodded.

"No, Marc. *You'll destroy us.*"

Randi made her way over to the boy's side and placed a hand on his shoulder. It trembled. "Where's your mom, Marc?"

"She left."

"What do you mean by 'left'?"

He shrugged. "She went to work one day and then never came home."

"How long ago?"

Lines of concentration appeared on his forehead. "A while ago. We were still in school."

Aubrey had been on break for at least a week. Maybe more.

"Eight days ago," Jayla said, rubbing Aiden's back.

Randi strode to the refrigerator and opened it up wide. Bare but for a near-empty jar of strawberry preserves and a box of baking soda. She opened the freezer. Empty. She opened the cabinets and found one with a bag of flour, a few spice containers, and the remnants of the tenth charity basket.

She stood there, unmoving for a full minute, her

throat tightening, tightening, tightening. Peering over her shoulder, she found Britt's gaze on her. She shook her head.

In a soft voice, Britt asked Jayla, "When did you run out of food?"

That one act of compassion was enough to release the girl's tension. Tears glided down her cheeks and her shoulders shook.

Aiden lifted his head and stared at his sister. "Don't cry, Jay-Jay." His little hands cupped her cheeks and gazed at her face as if his will alone could force away his sister's hurt.

"Three days ago," Marc interjected.

No wonder they'd taken the baskets. Desperate people did desperate things. She was a twelve-year-old girl, trying to keep her little family alive. What would've happened had they not come in contact with the baskets? What would've happened when the rent came due again? What would've happened when someone unsavory noticed they were no longer under adult supervision?

Randi couldn't bear to travel down that path any farther. Thank goodness Britt had asked for Marc's help this morning.

"What do we do now?" Randi asked.

"Our compromise is out," Maggie said. "We'll take the kids into custody."

Fear mottled Marc's face as he came to stand near his sister and brother.

"No more stalling, Jayla," Maggie said in a gentle, but firm voice. "Go pack a bag."

Randi's throat constricted all over again to see desperation enter the girl's gaze as she glanced at each adult, searching for help, for salvation, for an end to their nightmare. When no one stepped forward, defeat settled on the young girl's shoulders and she moved to put Aiden on the floor.

"Here, I'll take him," Randi said, holding out her hands.

Jayla hesitated and Aidan stared at her out-stretched hands with uncertainty.

"It's okay," Randi said. "Aiden, would you like to run down to the café with me for a brownie?"

Aiden scrubbed the back of his hand across his runny nose and leaned toward her.

When his warm, trembling body settled against her, something precious swarmed in her chest.

She caught Jayla's eye. "Meet us in the café?"

The girl produced a short, miserable nod before shuffling into her bedroom.

Britt strode over to Marc and pried the small backpack from the boy's fingers. He grasped his shoulder. "You did the right thing. Very brave of you."

"Jayla will never forgive me." Marc made no attempt to fight, simply allowed Britt to guide him out of the apartment.

The Robbins family left their home behind and marched into an abyss of uncertainty and fear and the knowledge that their lives would never be the same.

12

THREE HOURS LATER, RANDI STOOD IN THE MIDDLE OF the wildlife center, sipping warm cider and trying to smile when a piece of her heart broke off with each passing minute. Never in a million years would she forget the look of misery on the kids' faces as they filed into the back of Maggie's squad car.

Hovering next to her, Britt snaked an arm around her. "How are you holding up?"

Once the wildfire victims started arriving at the center, Randi had managed to put the kids' crisis in the background so she could focus on bringing joy to these families, even if only for a few hours. She'd also produced a respectable speech while distributing the donated items. And the raffle for the baskets had brought in nearly five thousand dollars. However, the biggest surprise of the night had been Jonah and Micki's announcement that they'd set up a GoFundMe campaign that had already hit over one hundred thousand dollars and was still climbing.

The Steele twins loved their behind-the-scenes secrets.

But no matter how much laughter filled the air around her, Randi couldn't shake the underlying reason they were all here, nor could she stop replaying the terrible events that had taken place only hours ago.

"So much sadness," she said.

"And kindness. Thanks to you."

"It doesn't seem like enough. A basket, a brownie. I should do more."

"You've done what you can. Just like every other volunteer in this room."

"If only I had a bazillion dollars like your brother, Jonah."

"It still wouldn't be enough. There will always be another natural disaster, another child in need. All the money in the world can't fix every challenge that comes up."

She leaned into his side. "I still can't believe Jayla took care of them for so long."

He kissed the top of her head. "Fearless. She reminds me of another woman who would do anything to protect the people she loved."

Tilting her head back, she kissed the side of his neck. "And of the young man who had to fill his father's shoes and take care of his brothers and sisters."

Her mountain man's face softened, and he leaned down to kiss her when something caught his eye.

Maggie approached, sans uniform. She wore her hair pulled back in a sleek ponytail and a soft, cream-colored sweater over skin-tight jeans tucked into knee-high, black leather boots. "Everything turned out great, Randi."

"Thank you. If nothing else, it gives them a few hours of joy before going back to the harsh realities of their lives."

"Speaking of harsh reality, I have some additional information if you'd like to hear it."

"About the kids?"

"More specifically their mother." Maggie studied her. "It can wait until tomorrow."

Randi pulled air into her lungs and forced a lighter expression on her face. "No, I'd rather hear what you have to say now."

"Let's move this conversation into my office," Britt said.

With Randi's hand in his, he led them down the corridor. He paused outside the secured administrative section of the center and drew his wallet out of his back pocket, waving it in front of a card reader. The red light turned green and a faint snick sounded. He pushed the door open and meandered his way around a grouping of desks until he reached his office.

The wall perpendicular to Britt's desk contained a bookcase filled with reference books. On each side of the bookcase were color photographs of the Steele-Shepherd red wolf pack. One of her favorites was a close-up of a pup from this year's litter—little Opal. Her crazy Yoda ears, dewy brown eyes, and fuzzy, golden-red mohawk made Randi smile every time.

Britt indicated a round table surrounded by four chairs that took up a good portion of his office. Made out of reclaimed barnwood, the set was gorgeous. "Have a seat."

Once everyone was settled, Maggie said, "After

hearing more about the Robbins's situation, we expanded our search."

"What did you find?" Randi asked.

"Mrs. Robbins is in a mental hospital."

Randi sat back, speechless.

"While Jayla was packing her bag, she shared with us that her mother had been sleeping a lot and crying nonstop. It sounded like depression to me. I had my team dig deeper, and they found a woman in Buncombe County, matching Mrs. Robbins's description, at Guardian Mental Health Center."

Randi couldn't imagine what it would be like to lose a husband and child within days of each other. She peered at Britt. Losing him alone would shatter her down to her core. But losing a child was unthinkable.

"Why didn't Mrs. Robbins make arrangements for her kids?" Randi asked.

"According to her doctor, the Asheville police found her wandering around their downtown area in the wee hours of the morning. She hasn't said a word since the police dropped her off. They didn't even know her name."

"Is she getting better?" Britt asked.

"Because of HIPAA, her doctor won't tell me much. They did say that she's shown some improvement, but didn't expect her to leave anytime soon."

"What's going to happen to the kids?"

"If we're unable to locate any relatives willing to give them shelter, we'll have to place them in foster care until their mother is deemed competent enough to take on the responsibility again."

"Foster care." Britt spat the words out as if he were spitting out a bug.

"Where are the kids now?"

"Kruger Children's Home."

"A group home," Randi whispered. She searched her brain for a better alternative, but she didn't know enough about the process. Helpless. She felt so damn helpless.

Britt wrapped her hand in his. The warmth calmed her spiraling thoughts, but did nothing to defrost the ice coating the inside of her veins.

"Could they stay with us?" he asked in a quiet voice.

Randi's gaze shot to his.

"Is that okay?" he asked.

Tears of love for this gruff, kind-hearted man rimmed her eyes. "Of course."

"You only have one bedroom in your cabin, Britt," Maggie said. "Where would they sleep?"

"They can have our bed tonight. Tomorrow we'll move everyone into Randi's bungalow. With Riley and Coen gone, it's sitting empty."

"They might visit for the holidays."

"I'm sure they won't mind using the cabin."

"Even so," Maggie said, "the bungalow only has two bedrooms."

"I'll add bunkbeds to the spare bedroom. It'll be fine."

"I don't know." She chewed on the inside of her cheek, clearly conflicted between her duty and her heart. "You're not a registered foster care family."

"Pull some strings," Britt said in a low, commanding voice.

Maggie raised a brow.

"Would you rather I talk to Grif?"

Maggie and Britt entered into a heated, bloody stare-down. Both were alphas. Both used to getting their way. Randi wasn't sure whose will would win out in the end.

"You know the kids staying with us would be better than putting them in the foster family system," Britt said.

"This isn't a weekend sleepover. Finding a relative willing to take on three kids could take a long time—if ever. They could be with you for months. Years, maybe."

Britt stared at her, unflinching.

More quietly, Maggie said, "You could grow to love them, only to have them taken away."

Britt glanced at Randi, and she nodded. "We'll deal with the future when it comes. Right now, the children's welfare is our priority."

Maggie rose. "I'll see what I can do. But I can't make any promises."

"Try hard, Maggie." Britt rose and wrapped his cousin in a hug. She hesitated a moment and then returned his affection. All was forgiven.

Maggie strode to the door, then glanced back. "I'll keep you posted."

"Thanks," they said in unison.

After Maggie's departure, Randi sat in stunned silence. In a matter of hours, she might be responsible for three scared and grieving children. Was she up for it? She didn't have a great role model in the way of parenting. Her father had died when she was young and her mother had rarely been home.

"I'm sorry," Britt said.

"Why?"

"I should have spoken to you in private. I put you on the spot."

"My thoughts were already wandering that way.

Did you make the offer for me? Or do you really want to do this?"

"They're good kids. They deserve something better than the foster care system."

"All of Maggie's influence might not be enough to persuade a judge to hand them over to us."

"Why not?"

"Because we're not married."

Britt stared at her for a long, contemplative moment.

Anxiety fluttered in her chest. "I'm not hinting, just stating a fact."

"Do you want to be married?"

"Do you?"

Britt reached into his jacket pocket and pulled out a small box. He cleared his throat. "I'd hoped to do this tonight, when we were alone by firelight and preferably naked."

Randi's mind sputtered out, froze from one breath to the next. *Is that a—?* Then her thoughts reignited, slammed into her from a million directions until a single word burst from her lips. "Yes."

He opened the case.

"Yes."

He got down on one knee.

"Yeesss."

His attention shifted to her face. "Yes?"

Her face split into a big grin. "Yes, I will marry you."

"OhmygodOhmygodOhmygod," Evie Steele squealed from the open office door. "Did you really just propose?" She took in her brother's position. "You did!" She rushed in and gave them both a hug. "Finally! I'm so happy for you both. Do you have a

date yet?" She bounced on her toes. "Mama and I will throw you a shower. It'll be so much fun—"

Evie's attention snapped between the two of them. "What?"

Britt held up the ring. "I'm not finished."

"Oh!" She waved him on. "Go ahead."

He raised an are-you-kidding-me brow.

Sobering, Evie said, "Would you like some privacy?"

"Yes, Squirt."

She hugged them both again before dashing away. At the door, she smiled and gave her big brother a watery wink. Then she was gone.

"Do you think she approves?" Randi asked, chuckling.

"I'm not sure. Should I call her back?"

"Not until you put that ring on my finger."

He slid the band of platinum and diamonds over her knuckle. "Will you marry me, Miranda Shepherd?"

Leaning forward, she touched her forehead to his. "With every beat of my heart."

"Do you remember my promise for what comes after the benefit?"

Anticipation made her inner muscles clench. "It's not over yet."

"Oh, yes, it is." He gave her a quick, hard kiss before grasping her hand and leading her through the admin area. He skirted the edge of the crowd, nodding to those who dared speak to two hundred pounds of muscle and determination plowing past them.

Smiling, Evie lifted her hand and waved. It was then that Randi noticed everyone in the center smiling in their direction. Britt's little sister hadn't wasted any time.

Right before Britt threw open the exit door, Randi lifted her ring finger in the air, smiling her head off. Sounds of clapping hands, laughter, and roars of congratulations followed in their wake.

Like two teenagers, she and Britt ran toward Old Blue. Toward their private *after* event.

EPILOGUE

ONE MONTH LATER.

CHEER UP, CHEER UP. CheerupCheerupCheerup.

Britt stirred from a deep sleep, blinking his scratchy eyes open. Predawn light filtered into the bedroom, casting everything in a milky glow.

The American robin continued its morning song as if it could raise the sun above the horizon one *Cheerup* at a time.

Randi lay facing him, her lips parted as sleep-drugged breaths filtered in and out. Due to an outbreak of influenza among her staff, she had been forced to work the late shift several times this week, not getting home until well past midnight.

A sixth sense burned between his shoulder blades and swept up his spine, leaving a trail of raised hairs. It was the age-old feeling of being watched. He craned his head around to his side of the bed and found Aiden standing there, staring at him, while holding his favorite stuffed panda in his arms.

"I'm thirsty," Aiden said.

Britt held a finger to his lips and peeled back the covers. Grabbing his jeans off a nearby chair, he held his hand out to Aiden and the two of them exited the bedroom.

He put his pants on and swung Aiden into his arms.

"Did you sleep okay, little man?"

"Uh-huh."

"Are you hungry?"

"Uh-huh."

Running the tap, Britt filled Aidan's sippy cup and then slid him into a chair at the table. "How about a banana while I fix us some breakfast?"

Aiden nodded. Even after a month of living with him and Randi, the five-year-old still spoke little.

He peeled a banana and cut it into bite-sized pieces before placing it on a plate in front of Aiden.

As quietly as he could, he began the morning ritual of making breakfast. Soon after the bacon and sausage began to sizzle, Jayla appeared in her Wonder Woman pajamas, wiping sleep from her eyes.

"Good morning," he said.

She yawned. "Morning."

Without being asked, Jayla pulled a container of precut fruit from the refrigerator and placed it on the table, then she grabbed the bread out of the bread box and dropped two slices into the toaster.

A few minutes later, Marc staggered into the kitchen and plopped down at the table. He bent forward, resting his head on his arms.

Britt gave the boy a few minutes to adjust to the early hour, then said, "How about you get the plates, Marc."

The boy groaned, but forced himself up and into action.

Smiling, Britt turned back to his eggs. Scrambled were Jayla and Aiden's favorite and sunny-side up for Marc.

"Should I wake Randi?" Jayla asked.

"Let her sleep. She didn't get home until early this morning."

"Will she have to work again tonight?"

Jayla had become quite attached to Randi.

"It's possible. The flu has hit Triple B hard."

The girl's face fell.

"Just a few more days, at the most."

"Did I hear my name?" Randi asked, pulling her hair back into a sloppy ponytail. She placed a kiss on the top of Aiden's head and against Marc's temple. Then she kissed Britt. "You should've woken me."

"You needed the sleep. Besides, I have excellent helpers."

Randi moved on to Jayla and opened her arms. The girl slid into her embrace with a contented sigh.

"Thank you for helping make breakfast."

"Welcome."

"It's Friday," Randi said. "Would you like to stop by the restaurant after school and help out?"

Jayla's eyes brightened and she straightened. "Yes!"

"Wonderful. Customers love it when you bring out their desserts."

"Can I come?" Marc asked.

"And me," Aiden mumbled around a banana bit.

"We'll all go," Britt said. "Marc, I'm ready for the plates."

After everyone had been served, they went

through their morning ritual of eating as a family and fighting over who gets the bathroom next. After the dust settled, Britt began wrangling them into their coats and backpacks.

"Say goodbye to Randi," Britt said.

Each child dutifully approached Randi, gave her a hug and kiss, and marched toward the garage.

When Britt bent to give Randi his kiss, he noticed tears sparkling in her eyes. "What's wrong?"

"It all feels so right, so normal, as if they were our children."

"But they're not."

"I know. It's just that—"

"I love them, too," he whispered. "But their mother could be well enough any day and come take them away."

"I know."

"They're ours for now," he said, "and we will love them and give them a safe and happy home."

"Yes." She brushed the backs of her fingers over his stubbled jaw. "Yes, we will."

A SIGN OF THE SEASON

STEELE RIDGE CHRISTMAS CAPER #2

KELSEY BROWNING

1

GRIF STEELE LOVED HIS HOMETOWN. EXCEPT WHEN HE hated it.

Headed toward the interstate for a winter weekend getaway, he and Carlie Beth almost made it all the way down Steele Ridge's Main Street. Almost. Then Camille Rafferty, the owner of the Mad Batter Bakery, dashed out in front of Grif's car and butterflied her arms overhead as if she were trying to flag down a rescue plane.

Grif's foot hovered over his brake but didn't press it.

Carlie Beth grabbed his arm. "You have to stop or you'll run her over."

"Which would dent Louise," he grumbled.

A surprised laugh popped from his wife's mouth. "You're horrible, you know that?"

But he wasn't. Not completely. Because he took a deep breath and came to a stop in the middle of Main. The bakery owner hurried to his driver's side, all the while making frantic roll-down-the-window motions with her hands.

"Do I have to?" he asked Carlie Beth.

"It's the holiday season. You know, goodwill and

kindness and all that," she said, pointing toward the festive "Happy Holidays!" banners his staff had recently ordered and hung. Still plenty of Christmas with the wreaths on every downtown door and green and red splashed everywhere, but Grif was committed to celebrating diversity in this town. "We have time for whatever this is."

Not in his mind, they didn't. Their reservation at a swanky and secluded mountain lodge began in an hour. Grif wanted to be there at three o'clock on the dot. He coveted every second of alone time he could get with his wife. Their daughters, Aubrey and Stella Grace, were thrilled to be spending their weekend with Grammy and Grampy, his parents, out at Tupelo Hill.

And he was thrilled to be spending his weekend in bed with his wife.

His very *naked* wife.

And right now, his hometown was damn well getting in the way of a weekend full of bare-assed debauchery and sexual shenanigans.

Still, he rolled down the window and slapped on his Steele Shark smile, the look that had both charmed reluctant clients and made more than one pro sports franchise owner pee their pants. "Hey, Carlie Beth and I were just on our way out of town. If this could wait until Monday, then—"

"It can't," the bakery owner hurried to say. "It absolutely can't."

Of course it couldn't.

"Then why don't you move out of the road, and I'll park so we can talk about whatever this is."

"Thank you." Her puckered forehead relaxed a little, and she hurried back to the sidewalk in front of the bakery, while Grif slowly and carefully parked

Louise, his beloved Maserati Quattroporte, between two empty spaces.

Carlie Beth shook her head. "Sometimes I think you love this car more than you do me."

He cut the engine and leaned over the console toward his wife. "She might've been my first love, but you, Carlie Beth Steele, will be my last." The kiss he gave her to prove his point was probably slightly more carnal than the town manager should've bestowed on his wife in public. *Screw it.* If the citizens here in Steele Ridge didn't like it, they could fire him.

Which sounded pretty damn good today, so he made sure his wife was thoroughly out of breath when he broke their kiss. Under her thin scoopneck sweater, her nipples were hard and poking against the fabric. He lifted his hand to touch, but she said, "Don't even think about it. If Maggie has to arrest us for public indecency, we'll be sitting in a jail cell this weekend instead of in a hot tub."

"Dammit." He gave her another quick kiss and pushed open his door. "I'll just be a second here."

As opposed to its normal crowd of customers, the sidewalk in front of the Mad Batter was deserted except for the owner standing there shifting from foot to foot. "How can I help you?" he asked her.

"It's gone," she said with a flourish of her arm.

Grif forced himself to breathe through his frustration and impatience to ask, "What's gone?"

"The sandwich sign," she said. "When I came in this morning, it wasn't here."

Excellent. This wasn't *his* problem. Theft was under his cousin's—Sheriff Maggie Kingston's—

purview. He pulled out his phone and dialed her direct number. "Mags, we've got a situation down at the Mad Batter. The sandwich sign is missing, so I need you to get someone on it ASAP."

What he didn't say was that the owner was going to have a sandwich-sign-induced stroke.

"Yeah, that's not going to happen," Maggie said, her voice full of cheer that wasn't holiday-induced. "We're operating with a light crew right now. Most of my people are in Charlotte for some advanced interview and interrogation training. I can't spare anyone for something that small."

"All you have to do is take the police report. You don't even have to..." He trailed off when the bakery owner's eyes narrowed. Yeah, he'd been about to say Maggie didn't even really have to follow up. That wasn't the attitude of a caring and effective city manager. And dammit, he did care.

Right now, he just cared a little more about getting laid.

"Why don't you take care of it?" Maggie asked him. "Someone probably just stowed it in the wrong storage closet."

"Carlie Beth and I are on our way out of town."

"Only takes ten minutes to check," Maggie said mildly. "How about I throw in a little incentive? I'll deputize you right here on the phone."

Oh no. She was not about to patronize him. He turned his back on the bakery owner and lowered his voice to say to his cousin, "This is the first weekend Carlie Beth and I have had completely alone since Stella Grace was born. Do you have any idea all the things I plan to do with and to my wife? Every minute is critical here, Mags."

She snorted a laugh. "Buck up, buddy. There are plenty of orgasms available in two days."

"One less every ten minutes," he said.

"Wow, you're an ambitious man, I'll give you that," Maggie said. "All you have to do is find the sign. Then you can have as much wild monkey sex as you can in the other forty-seven hours and fifty minutes."

"I'll remember this," he warned. "As Jay's sports agent, I can book him so many endorsement gigs that you'll never see him."

At his mention of her pro football boyfriend, Maggie just laughed. "You can try, but he can refuse. Which I will insist that he do."

Damn her for being right. He disconnected and turned to the bakery owner. "How about we take a look around inside? I bet someone simply misplaced the sign."

"I've already checked everywhere. Besides, Jeanine said she accidentally left it outside yesterday when she closed up. Anyone could've taken it."

Not the best time of year for the baker's assistant to be careless like that. Steele Ridge was a small North Carolina mountain town, but they still had some crime now and again. And this was just the kind of prank that would appeal to high-schoolers or the college kids who were home on winter holiday break. If that were the case, that sandwich sign was now propped in some teenager's bedroom like a trophy.

It was a goner.

Which actually made Grif's life a little easier. He reached for his wallet. "Then it's probably long gone by now. Why don't I just buy the bakery a replacement?"

Her mouth dropped open, and she bug-eyed him. "Absolutely not. That sign was special made just for the Mad Batter. It's the only one we've ever used. It's the only one Jeanine can or will write her messages on."

Yeah, the baker's assistant was actually pretty famous for her sometimes pithy, always insightful, prophecies. But it was just a damn sign. "I'll go in and talk with Jeanine. She'll understand."

"You can't. She was so upset that I had to send her home." She hooked a thumb back toward the bakery windows. "Which hasn't been a problem today since we've only had about ten percent of our normal foot traffic."

Damn. The empty sidewalk outside hadn't been a fluke. Normally at this time of year, the Mad Batter was filled with both locals and tourists clamoring for their holiday treats like Christmas monkey bread and gingerbread cake. "And you think the lack of customers has something to do with the missing sign?" If so, she had every right to be upset.

"I know it does. Please, Grif, I need this sign back."

He sighed. He'd always told the town's business owners that he had their backs. His ideas and incentives had brought back—and would hopefully continue to bring—business to Steele Ridge. He couldn't abandon them just because he wanted hot sex with his wife. He glanced at his watch. "I can help for a couple of hours. If we don't find it by then, we'll pick up the search on Monday."

She threw her arms around him and squeezed him like a hungry anaconda. "I have faith you'll find it."

And Grif had faith he would have his wife under him this afternoon.

He turned toward his car where Carlie Beth was waiting and waved for her to get out.

She stepped out. "What's going on?"

Speedbump. That's all. He tried to smile at his wife, but it felt more like a grimace on his face. "Apparently, if we want to have sex, we have to first find a missing sandwich sign."

2

ONLY IN STEELE RIDGE.

Carlie Beth chuckled at her husband's two-year-old-without-a-lollipop expression, but realistically, a missing sandwich sign from the Mad Batter was no laughing matter. She buttoned up the teal wool coat Grif had given her when the chill first hit the North Carolina mountains in the fall. It was way too fancy for her, with its fine fabric and intricately decorated buttons. But damned if she didn't love this coat.

But not nearly as much as she loved her husband. And although they'd only truly been together since Grif moved back to Steele Ridge within the past few years, she'd loved this man since the night their first daughter was conceived on the hood of a Ford Taurus.

"So you're saying Jeanine's sign is gone?" she asked him.

"Yeah, probably snatched by some kids. And unless some nosy parent finds it in their kid's room, we're probably shit outta luck. But Camille is having a conniption fit over it. And Maggie doesn't have anyone to send over right now. She *deputized* me."

He said the word with such disgust that Carlie

Beth couldn't help but grab him by the coat collar and pull him close. She made sure to put as much seduction into her voice as she could muster when she said, "Well, well then. I have always had a thing for men in law enforcement. You solve this case, and there might be a bonus coming your way."

"Cop lover, huh?"

"Three words for you. Detective Elliot Stabler."

"You're yanking my chain," he said. "But I'm gonna roll with it for now."

"Any ideas of where to start?" This was actually kind of exciting. She'd never had any interest in law enforcement before, but her heart was pumping faster at the thought of tracking down the sign thief.

"I tried to just give Camille money for a new sign, but she wasn't having it."

Carlie Beth sighed. Sometimes her husband and his youngest brother Jonah thought any problem could be solved by tossing enough money at it. "There are some things a wad of cash can't replace."

Grif swept a gentle hand over her face and cupped her cheek. "You think I don't know that? I tried to buy you off once and it didn't go over too well."

The memory of the check Grif had once written to her, trying to bargain his way into Aubrey's life, still made Carlie Beth a bit queasy. Up to that point, she'd never seen so many zeroes on something she could've deposited into her bank account. She hadn't taken it. She and Grif still didn't share a bank account. Not because Grif hadn't tried, but because the zeroes he made as a big-time sports agent overwhelmed Carlie Beth.

"Then I suggest we start in the obvious place," she said, taking Grif's hand. "Inside the bakery."

He gave her hand a playful squeeze. "You just want hazelnut cream cheese puffs, don't you?"

"Hey, if some happen to jump into a Mad Batter sack and make it into my hands, I'm not going to reject them. That would be rude. No hazelnut cream cheese puff should ever go unloved."

As they walked toward the bakery's entrance, Grif said, "You loved plenty of them when you were pregnant with Stella Grace." So much that Grif swore their baby had come out of the womb smelling slightly of hazelnuts.

"I can't stroll by this place with her without her making gimme-grabby-hands toward the bakery windows." Especially now that the windows were decorated with faux snow and an entire painted gingerbread village.

"That time you tried to fool her with a bran muffin didn't go over too well." Grif held open the door for Carlie Beth.

"I should've known she was way too smart for that." The scents drifted over her—nuts, cinnamon, vanilla, sugar. All the flavors that made life worth living. But this time, none of them made Carlie Beth crave baked goods. In fact, her stomach seemed to shrink in response. She tried to concentrate on the music instead—cheerful "Little Saint Nick" by the Beach Boys. *Run run reindeer... but you stay put, Carlie Beth.*

"They're okay, right?"

"Who?"

Grif came to a standstill and gawked at her. "Who do you think? Our girls!"

She wanted to shake her head at him, but she smiled instead. "Of course they are. Your mom and dad were over the moon to have them for the weekend. They'll be so spoiled by the time we get back to Steele Ridge that they probably won't want to come home with us."

Grif spun toward the door. "Then we're going to pick them up right now."

For a man who'd been shocked—and more than a little pissed—to find out he was a father, Grif Steele had become Super Dad, right down to the tricked-out minivan.

Carlie Beth dug in her heels and held tightly to his hand. "I'm joking. They will have a wonderful time with your parents, but they're *both* daddy's girls. You don't have to worry about them tossing you over for someone else."

He reached into his coat pocket. "Maybe I should just call Mom and—"

"Uh-uh." Carlie Beth snagged the phone and dropped it into her own pocket. "We have a sandwich sign to find and then a weekend of sexy times ahead of us."

Still, her husband was frowning, which meant she needed to up the ante a little. Carlie Beth rose on tiptoe and whispered in his ear, "I bought a bag full of killer underwear for this weekend. Don't make me use it on someone else."

His eyes widened. "You? My wife who wears flannel shirts and work boots? You bought lingerie?"

"Don't look so shocked."

"*You* bought it?"

Damn him for knowing her so well. "Brynne and Tessa helped a little."

"Thank God," he sighed.

"Thanks for having such faith in me." She gave him a friendly punch in the arm. "Keep it up, buster, and you won't get within ten feet of all that lace and stuff."

His face took on a serious and stubborn cast. She knew that expression. It meant he was ready to get down to business and would come out on top of whatever challenge was in front of him. "We'll go table by table."

Unfortunately, only four of the bakery's tables were occupied. Even mid-afternoon, the Mad Batter usually held a full house. Still, Grif cranked up his Steele Shark smile and approached an older couple. "Mr. and Mrs. Trambly! It's great to see you both."

Carlie Beth hid her own smile because she knew exactly what Grif was doing. The Tramblys were two of the biggest gossips in town next to old Jacob Greene. If they heard about the missing sign, everyone in Steele Ridge would know within the hour.

Grif continued, "It seems the Mad Batter has a little problem that I was hoping you could help me with."

At that, Mrs. Trambly put down her fork next to a half-eaten piece of lemon cake and looked at him over her bifocals. "Anything for you, Griffin. How can we help?"

"It seems that someone has taken the sandwich sign from outside. Have you, by any chance, heard anything about who might've played a prank like this?"

Mrs. Trambly frowned. "I mentioned to my husband that it was odd not to see it on the sidewalk, but I didn't realize it had been stolen. How horrible."

Carlie Beth had a feeling the woman's frown had less to do with the missing sign than it did with the fact that she'd apparently missed any scuttlebutt about the theft. She asked Mr. Trambly, "What about you? Have you heard or seen anything?"

The older man's eyes widened and he darted a quick look in his wife's direction as if to say he would never risk admitting to her that he knew something she didn't. "No. Absolutely not."

Grif pulled out a business card and a pen. He jotted down his cell number and slid the card toward the Tramblys. "Would you please call me immediately if you hear anything?"

"You can count on us. We'll find this sign in no time." Mrs. Trambly fluttered her fingers toward the high-school girl behind the counter. "Honey, can we get a couple of to-go boxes over here?"

As she and Grif headed for the next table, Carlie Beth said, "You did that on purpose."

"Yep," he said cheerfully. "Why do all the work yourself when you can delegate?"

3

GRIF APPROACHED THE NEXT TABLE AND TRIED NOT TO let the impatience streaming through him show on his face. "Mr. Felder, does that apple fritter taste as good as it looks?"

"Mad Batter always does 'em best and..." And safer, Grif thought. Thomas Felder was known for his cooking mishaps, so it was safer for everyone when he ate out.

"I don't suppose you heard what I was talking with the Tramblys about, did you?"

Mr. Felder wiped his mouth. "I don't meanta eavesdrop, but..."

But eavesdropping was a way of life in a small town. Sometimes a total pain in the ass. Other times, a blessing. "If you know anything, it would be a huge help."

"Well, I noticed a little something the other day..." He trailed off.

Carlie Beth squeezed Grif's hand as if she instinctively understood that his keeping-his-shit-together wouldn't withstand Mr. Felder continuing to use incomplete sentences. "It's so wonderful to have people here in town keeping their eyes on everything," Carlie Beth said. "What did you notice?"

"Well, that sandwich sign looked like it could use a new coat of paint. I mentioned it to Jeanine. Even offered to paint it myself for free. But she just looked at me like I'd suggested chopping it up for firewood."

This could be good. The break they needed. "But being a stand-up guy, you saw it last night and took it home to paint it."

Unfortunately, Mr. Felder shook his head. "Nuh-uh. No way. If I took that sign without Jeanine's okay, she'd skin me alive. Worse yet, she'd write some message on that board, and I'd keel over dead the next day."

Well, crap. "Have you heard anyone else talking about the sign?" Grif asked. "Maybe some kids joking about stealing it?"

"I would've set them straight if that was the case."

"Thanks for your time, Mr. Felder." Grif took out another business card, and although it pained him, wrote out his cell number. At this rate, the entire town would have access to him 24/7. "If you hear anything, give me a shout."

Mr. Felder gave him a snappy salute. "Will do."

"Damned dead ends," Grif grumbled as he and Carlie Beth left Mr. Felder's table.

"Maybe," she said. "Maybe not."

"What do you mean?"

"I'm thinking," she said. "Let's go ahead and talk with everyone here before I give you my theory."

If she knew where the sign was, she should tell him now. "Carlie Beth…"

"Grif…"

Damn. Now they were doing it. "Tell me what you're thinking, and I'll buy you a dozen hazelnut cream cheese puffs."

Carlie Beth's face went a little pale and she put her hand over her mouth. "That's... that's okay. I'm not really hungry right now."

Yeah, she said that, but he knew his wife. He'd get a box and she'd be halfway through them before they made it to their suite at the romantic mountain inn he'd booked for the weekend.

Still, they talked with the folks at the other two tables without gaining the tiniest hint of what might've happened to the bakery sign. Grif checked his watch. He'd told Camille he'd give the search two hours. It had only been twenty minutes, and he was jumping out of his skin.

Carlie Beth had packed sexy lingerie. For a woman who was a die-hard cotton fan, this was a BFD. "What color?" he asked her.

She stared up at him. "You know that sign is red with gold leaf."

"Not the damn sign. The stuff Brynne and Tessa picked out for you."

"Really, Grif? You can't wait and find out for yourself?"

"I need some motivation here."

"Brynne called them jewel tones."

"Are you wearing them now?" He hadn't thought anything of it when she shooed him out of their bedroom so she could pack. Now he wished he'd done a little spying and eavesdropping of his own.

"Would you like me to unbutton my shirt so you can see for yourself?" A tiny smile lifted her lips.

"Yes," he said automatically, then looked around

at the folks munching on baked goods and watching Carlie Beth and him. "I mean no, dammit."

But she'd definitely given him motivation to find that sign. "Give me a second here," he told her before striding up to the counter and ordering a box of hazelnut cream cheese puffs. While the clerk packed them up, he asked, "Have you seen anyone paying special interest to the sandwich sign lately?"

"Nope," she said. "I'm just here for a few days while I'm on winter break. This is the first shift I've worked since the summer."

"No friends who might take it as a joke?"

"None of my friends are stupid enough to risk Jeanine's prophetic payback."

Smart kids. He handed her a twenty and tucked the bakery box under his arm. "Keep the change."

The clerk's smile reminded him of Aubrey's when he inevitably said yes to something she wanted.

He ushered his wife out the door and she stared at the box he held. "I told you I wasn't hungry."

"We'll have them later, then." He was already imagining finger-painting the custard all over Carlie Beth's body. And the two bits of pastry would perfectly cover her nipples. Grif's stomach growled. They needed to get on the road. "You said you had an idea about where the sign might be."

"Mr. Felder said it needed to be painted."

"But Jeanine wouldn't let him do it."

"Bless Mr. Felder's heart, but he's not known for his attention to detail and that would be important to Jeanine."

Yeah, Mr. Felder's tendency to wander away from a project was exactly what Grif had been thinking about earlier. One time, the old guy was frying catfish and Grif's cousin Cash had been the firefighter to put out the resulting kitchen fire. Grif had heard Felder's house still stunk of fish guts, and on a windy day, the neighbors always called Grif's office to complain.

How had his life come to this?

Nah, it was okay. Because his life now included Carlie Beth, Aubrey, and Stella Grace. He could handle a few fish guts complaints if it meant having his own family and being close to his parents, brothers, and sisters.

"There might be monkeys loose in my circus," he muttered to himself. "But at least I have a circus and most of the time, I love my circus."

Carlie Beth laughed. "What in the world are you talking about?"

"You and the girls."

"So you're saying we're monkeys?"

Grif rubbed a weary hand across his forehead. "I'm saying I love my life even if it makes me crazy sometimes."

"So now we're *crazed* monkeys?"

"I can't dig myself out of this, can I?"

"You don't have a shovel big enough." By this time, her smile was wide and mocking.

"For the sake of our weekend, can we pretend I didn't say any of that? Can we just find the sign and go have sex?"

"I used to think you were slick and charming," Carlie Beth said mildly.

Oh, if they could just get the hell out of town, he would charm her into being the slick one. But he knew better than to crack that joke right now. Not after the circus monkeys. Shit, he was turning into his brother Reid.

No filter.

You can do better, Steele.

He lifted his wife's hand, looked into her gorgeous brown eyes, and said, "Carlie Beth, I love you. And wanting to spend the weekend showing you all the ways I love you is making me a bumbling idiot. Can you forgive me?" He kissed her palm.

"Maybe you haven't lost all your charm," she said. "But you will still pay for this conversation later."

He grinned at her. "I will absolutely drop to my knees and beg for forgiveness." He would also make her scream and she knew it. That was another thing about married-with-family sex—it needed to be modulated, and he wanted to hear his wife let loose.

"Fine," she huffed. "Mr. Felder pointed out that the sign needed painting. Maybe someone else overheard that and decided to surprise Jeanine with a new paint job."

Completely plausible in this town. "Okay. I can get behind that."

"So I'm thinking we hit Cohen and Son Signs first. If it's not there, then we can move on and talk with anyone who sells painted items at the farmer's market. And if that's a bust, then maybe we check the auto body place out on the interstate?"

Yeah, he liked that. Because if they were on the interstate, then they would be headed out of town. Grif opened the car door and hustled Carlie Beth inside. "Watch out, Sheriff Maggie Kingston. Detective Carlie Beth is on the case."

4

SHE HAD TO HAND IT TO HER HUSBAND. HE HADN'T lost his shit. Yet. But if they didn't track down this sign soon, he would lose his patience. He didn't do it often, but when he did? He was scarier than Reid on a rampage.

She needed to soothe the savage beast a little, so she pointed at the holiday lights forming a canopy over the Main Street buildings. "Every year, this town gets a little more festive during the holidays, and most of that is thanks to you and your staff. Stella Grace loved the big tree lighting this year. And the new banners, I just adore them."

"I know what you're doing," he said.

"No one is immune to flattery as a form of distraction."

"Keep it up until we're out of town, and I'll make it worth your while."

They parked in front of Cohen & Son Signs, not far from the bakery, just a couple streets off Main. The holiday decor wasn't as abundant here, but this block had obviously coordinated the use of blue and silver garland made of tiny snowflakes and menorahs. The Cohen family had owned the sign business for as long as Carlie Beth could remember. Used to be, they'd paint signs for all the businesses in town, but these days, they seemed to do a lot more banners and graphic design.

Sign of the times. Ha.

Carlie Beth popped out of the car because the rich scent of those hazelnut cream cheese puffs had been almost unbearable, even on the short drive from the Mad Batter.

Do not get sick. You don't want to ruin this weekend.

She and Grif walked inside the sign shop to find Chip Cohen clicking away on a computer and whistling off-key. He looked up and smiled at them. "Hey there. HowcanIhelpya?" His face quickly sobered. "No problems with the holiday banners, is there, Mr. Steele?"

The shop had produced the gorgeous banners that hung from signposts up and down Main Street. Each one showcased a different symbol of the season, from a kinara candleholder to a dreidel to the star of David to old Saint Nick.

"No," Grif told him. "That's not why we're here."

His smile firmly back in place, Chip hopped up from his stool and walked toward them. "Well, I'm always happy to do work for the city manager."

"Actually," Carlie Beth said, "we're hoping you were already doing some work."

"Uh. If someone from the city ordered something else, I don't know anything about it."

"Your dad still paints hand-lettered signs, doesn't he?" she asked.

"Yeah, and there's been more call for it lately since business has picked up around town, but we don't have any projects like that going right now."

"No one happened to bring by the Mad Batter's sandwich sign and asked to have it repainted?"

"Lemme give Dad a holler and double-check, but I don't think so."

Chip made the call and after a few disheartening questions and grunts, he hung up. "Naw. He's not seen hide nor hair of that sign."

Well, crap. She turned to find Grif scowling. "We'll find it," she assured him.

Grif asked Chip, "Think your dad could build and paint a sign just like it?"

"Well, it being around the holidays and all, we're kinda backed up and Dad's no spring chicken. If I had to guess, I'd say it'd be January before he could get to it. And something like that's gotta be built from the ground up. Prob'ly take a good six weeks."

Carlie Beth said to Grif, "Camille will lose her mind if it takes that long."

Chip hurried to say, "Now we don't want her taking her business elsewhere. What if we could promise it by mid-January?"

If the lack of foot traffic was any indication, the bakery couldn't wait even that long.

"How about I get back to you on that?" Grif said.

When they returned to the car, the sweet cream puff scent swept over Carlie Beth. Grif immediately reached into the backseat for the box and shoved it toward her. "I bet you want one of these now."

Oh, no. No, she did not. Carlie Beth breathed through her mouth and pushed away the box. "I'm not feeling a hundred percent right now. Why don't you take those inside and give them to Chip?"

"But—"

"Now, Grif."

He was out of the car and back in the driver's

seat in under a minute. His eyebrows lowered, he turned to Carlie Beth and ran a hand over her hair. "What's wrong?"

She shrugged out of her coat and fanned herself. "I think I just got overheated and it hit me the wrong way. I'll be fine."

"You sure?"

Before she could answer one way or another, Grif's phone rang and he answered it on speaker. "Are the girls okay, Mom?"

"Of course they are," Joan Steele said, a laugh in her voice. "We're baking cookies and dancing to Aubrey's latest Apple Music playlist."

"Did we forget to bring something that Stella Grace needs? You have a key to the house, so you can just—"

"Stella Grace is just fine. If your dad has played one game of Ride-a-Little-Horsey with her, he's done it twenty times. Every time the rider falls down, Stella Grace laughs like she's never experienced it before. But my question is why you and Carlie Beth are still in town. I've had no less than four people call and tell me they saw you."

Grif groaned and rested his forehead on the steering wheel. Carlie Beth stroked his back, trying to comfort him. He told his mom, "The Mad Batter's sign is missing."

"That's bad," Joan said. "And I guess you got caught up in the middle of it."

"Mags is short-staffed today."

"You're a good boy, Griffin."

If his mother could've seen the glare he shot at his phone for her comment, she would have taken a wooden spoon to his backside. So Carlie Beth spoke up. "We'll look one or two more places, and if we don't find it, the situation will have to wait until next week."

"That's reasonable," Joan said. "Then I'll hang up and let you get back to the search."

Grif hit end call and looked at Carlie Beth. "Please tell me you have some brilliant idea about where this damn thing is."

She didn't, but her stomach knew that she needed a vomit emission containment device and soon. "Can you drive us to the Murchison building?"

5

GOD ALMIGHTY! CARLIE BETH'S FACE WAS THE COLOR of mold, so Grif put the car in reverse, backed out of the parking space, and hit the gas. When they made it to the building that housed his office and an up-stairs apartment he'd once lived in, his wife lurched out of the car and through the front door. She didn't lift a hand to wave at his small staff, just stumbled her way to the first-floor bathroom and slammed the door behind her.

Knowing she probably wouldn't want anyone to hear whatever was going on behind that closed door, he said loudly, "So how are the contracts coming for Mountain SpringFest?"

"Really?" his newly hired assistant James asked. "Do you trust us so little that you couldn't leave town without checking up on us one more time?"

It was true that Grif wasn't the best delegator in the world. That came from years of conducting one-on-one negotiations for multimillion-dollar con-tracts. With that much money on the line, it had al-ways been "In Grif We Trust," but things were different now.

He waved his staff into a huddle and lowered his

voice. "I didn't have any plans to stop by here, but Carlie Beth's not feeling too great."

"Oh." His assistant's eyebrows went up. He knew how much Grif had been looking forward to this weekend. They weren't exactly BFFs, but men knew why other men took women away on romantic weekends. "Oh no. Do you think she caught the bug that's been going around?"

Lord, he hoped not. Because if that was the case, they would be spending the weekend at home with Grif fetching Carlie Beth a trashcan and a six-pack of ginger ale. "Don't even say those words," he gritted out.

"Sorry. Jesus. Sorry." Grif's assistant hurried over to a kitchenette they'd built into a corner of the main room. From the fridge, he pulled out a can of ginger ale. "Maybe offer her this?"

Smart man. Exactly why Grif had hired him after he graduated from Duke. He wouldn't keep him long. The guy had a bright future ahead of him, but Grif would teach him and get good work from him while he could. He took the ice-cold soda and approached the bathroom door. "Shortcake, I've got a cold drink out here for you. Can you let me in?"

The toilet flushed and the water ran for several seconds before the door opened a crack, showing one brown eye and a sliver of her pale face.

"Do you think you can make it upstairs?" he asked. Sometimes the apartment had a tenant, like when Emmy McKay was living there, but it was empty at the moment. "Maybe lie down for a few minutes until this thing passes?" *Please, please let it pass.*

"That's probably a good idea," she croaked out.

He wrapped his arm around her and led her

slowly up the stairs. And it said something about her state when she immediately flopped down on the ass-ugly green, pink, and yellow couch Hattie Martin had once owned. She and her husband were rumored swingers, so Grif had never been sure of the contamination level of those cushions. He kept meaning to get a cover for the thing. Or better yet, an entirely new couch.

But he'd also become somewhat attached to the damn thing. It was an eyesore, but it had played a small part in several relationships around this town. He'd heard that his cousin Cash was especially fond of it.

Carlie Beth's eyes were closed, making it clear that Grif now had a much bigger problem than a missing bakery sign.

He knelt next to the couch and picked up her limp hand. "Maybe we should get you home."

One eye eased open. "Just give me a few minutes. A couple of sips of ginger ale and I'll be fine." Both eyes were open now, and she took the soda from him. "Do you think there's any food in here?"

"You didn't want the cream puffs fifteen minutes ago."

"I know." She popped the top on the can and took a small sip. "But I'm starting to feel better already. Something salty."

"James usually has some popcorn downstairs."

"Perfect," she said. "I'll be good to go by the time you get back up here with it."

Yeah, they'd just see about that, but in his mind, Grif had already replaced champagne and strawberries with ginger ale and saltines.

· · ·

CARLIE BETH TOOK A FEW MORE SIPS OF THE GINGER
ale, letting it do its fizzy magic on her stomach. This
wasn't at all what she'd had in mind for this weekend. But she knew if she could just get a little food,
she'd be fine.

Poor Grif. His turned-down lips made it clear he
believed their weekend was a total bust.

Hm... Maybe she needed to show him he was
wrong.

After all, it wasn't as if that sandwich sign was
going anywhere.

Soda in hand, she pushed herself off the couch.
Checked her palm for any sign that any of its icki-
ness had rubbed off on her. She smiled to herself.
Maybe it had, but she was not going to use that
couch the way it had been used in the past. A
woman had her standards.

But she had very good—excellent, in fact—
memories of another spot in this apartment. In the
bedroom, she closed the window shades, stripped
down to her bra and panties, and draped her clothes
over a side table. Then she boosted herself up onto a
sill of one of the windows, that faced Main Street.

Oh, yeah. She was feeling better already, a tingle
of anticipation buzzing between her legs and
through her breasts. A handful of that popcorn Grif
had promised and she'd be ready to roll.

The apartment door opened, and Grif called out,
"Carlie Beth, where are you? Are you okay?"

She was about to be way better than okay. With
the skills her husband brought to the bedroom, in
twenty minutes, she would be marvelous. "In here."

"Dammit, you were sick again, weren't you?" He
rushed into the hallway, his gaze immediately going
to the bathroom. When he realized the door was

open and she wasn't inside, he turned toward the bedroom.

His attention landed on the windowsill where Carlie Beth was sitting, and the bag of popcorn in his hand dropped, precious kernels escaping and landing on the wooden floor. "Wha..."

Oh, she loved it when she was able to surprise him. She mimicked Stella Grace's gimme-grabby hands. "I need that popcorn."

"Wha..."

"You're obviously not capable of speaking, but if you could get your legs to work and bring me that popcorn, I would really appreciate it." She arched her back a little to entice him. The pushup bra Brynne and Tessa had recommended was doing its job, making Carlie Beth's girls look at least a size bigger. Heck, the cleavage she was sporting today was even turning her on.

Without ever taking his gaze from her, Grif scooped up the bag and zombie-walked toward her. "I thought you were feeling sick."

"All better now."

"So you basically had the twenty-minute stomach bug?"

"Guess so." She snagged the bag from him and tossed a few pieces of popcorn into her mouth. Oh, yes. Salty, buttery goodness. "Don't guess there's any sriracha in the building, is there?"

He cocked his head and studied her. "I can go back downstairs and check."

"No worries." Even without the spicy addition, she ate a couple of handfuls and was absolutely back on her game. She smiled at her husband.

"What's going on here?" he asked.

She laughed. "If you don't know that, then we

have bigger problems than a missing sandwich sign."

He winced. "Don't remind me."

Grabbing him by the coat collar, she pulled him close and bracketed her knees on either side of his hips. It was obvious that even though Grif's brain might not have caught up, his body was an over-achiever. His erection showed a promising outline against his jeans. "This would work much better if you were naked," she said, leaning in to trail kisses up his neck.

"Are you sure about this?"

Her husband, the gentleman. She took his hand and placed it between her legs, pressing his palm against the silky softness of her panties. "Does it feel like I'm sure?"

"Jesus." He rubbed up and down, the friction so wonderful that she widened her legs. Unfortunately, Grif stepped back, taking his hand with him.

"Hey, you. Where are you going?"

"To get the hell out of all these clothes and spend a little time looking at you in that underwear. Remind me to send flowers to Brynne and Tessa. Expensive flowers. Lots and lots of expensive flowers."

Carlie Beth laughed. She and Grif might be married with a family now, but this man could always, would always, make her laugh.

Grif stripped off his coat and tossed it aside, not even watching to see where it would land. It hit the edge of the bed and slid to the floor. Her sartorially splendid husband, in his expensive jeans and cashmere sweater, was more interested in her than his wardrobe. An excellent sign.

He crossed his arms and pulled off his sweater, leaving his chest bare.

"Come back here," she said.

"I still have clothes on."

"Just for a second."

He did as she asked, and Carlie Beth ducked her head to gently bite his left nipple.

"Holy fuck!"

One tongue flick and she did the same to his other nipple. Drawing back and grinning at him, she said, "I just wanted to make sure you were on board."

"If I were any more on board, I'd be able to use my board to build an entire house."

"Then lemme see whatcha got."

Grif toed out of his shoes and shoved down his jeans and boxers. Yes, he was absolutely on board, his erection hard against his stomach.

"I'll take one of those, please." She pointed at his cock and fluttered her eyelashes the best she could.

"You'll take this one more than once."

"How about we save all the rest of them when we're at the lodge?"

Grif took himself in hand and gave his penis two strong strokes. "Why don't you tell me about all the rest of them. You know, just to keep me motivated."

"You look plenty motivated to me."

Grif's eyes softened as he looked at her, his gaze going to the top of her head, pausing appreciatively at her unusually bodacious bosom, over her stomach, between her legs, and down them. "You are so beautiful, Carlie Beth."

She wasn't. Not like some of the women she knew he'd dated when he lived out in LA. But she'd learned to appreciate herself and her body. She might be built like a tomboy, but her hair was a gorgeous strawberry blond and she was vain enough to keep it long. And it didn't take big breasts and curvy hips for sex to be good. It merely took hitting the right switch in a woman's brain.

"I guess this means you like the lingerie?"

"I *love* it. Almost as much as I love you."

"If you're nice to me, maybe you'll find some more of it under the Christmas tree."

"How about you wrap it up and leave it in the bedroom?"

Before Grif, she'd been all-cotton granny panties. But for him, she was trying to up her game. Strangely, she'd found that sexy undies weren't all butt crawlers. Some of them were actually comfortable as well as girlie. A miracle. "How about you come over here and unwrap *me*?"

6

————

CARLIE BETH MUST BE JUST AS CONVINCED THEY WERE never going to make it out of town for their weekend getaway if she was initiating memory lane sex on the windowsill. Granted, that was his favorite windowsill ever, but he'd had in mind big-cushy-bed sex, hot-tub sex, and maybe a little in-front-of-the-fireplace sex.

But he wasn't stupid, and he was still a man. So he went to his wife and kissed her.

Gently at first. Soft and slow and sweet. Seduction was never a bad thing.

But Carlie Beth had something else altogether in mind. She grabbed him by the hair, manacled her legs around his hips, and pulled him in. And kissed the holy fuck out of him.

Apparently, she was as turned on by her new lingerie as he was. And time *was* a factor here. Speed did not have to dictate quality. But it could impact satisfaction.

Grif let his hands drop to her hips and he tugged on the teal-colored lace he found there. Carlie Beth dropped her legs and lifted one butt cheek and then the other so he could work her panties down her legs. The scrap of fabric caught and dangled around her right ankle. She tried to shake it loose, but he whispered, "Leave it."

He didn't bother to open the clasp on her pretty bra. Just pulled down the cups and let her breasts pop free. He took a second to admire his work. The band and Carlie Beth's heavy breathing plumped up her breasts. Grif grabbed her ass and yanked her forward on the windowsill.

Taking a breast in hand, he looked into his wife's eyes and smiled. "I like you like this."

"With foam-cup enhanced boobs?"

"No, I like you panting"—he dropped his other hand between her legs and slipped his finger along the softness there—"and wet." And when he slid two fingers inside her, Carlie Beth's eyes drooped closed and she arched her back on a moan.

He worked her and watched her. Every stroke and slide softening her face and body until she was tuned in only to what he was doing to her. When her hips began a restless dance against his hand, he knew she was close. So he replaced his hand with his mouth and gave her clit one strong suck.

"HolyJesus!" she screamed along with some nonsensical syllables that may or may not have included more religious figures and heaven.

Grif grinned against her inner thigh and gave it a tiny nip and soothing kiss for good measure.

When he stood, she slumped against him. "Pretty sure I saw the face of God," she murmured.

"I don't even know what to say to that."

Rather than reply, she wrapped her arms around him and widened her knees. All the invitation he needed to slide inside her heat. And it didn't matter how many times he'd shared bodies with this woman, it always made his world balanced and right. Always felt like a homecoming.

Grif kissed her neck and began to rock against her. Her breasts brushed against his chest. Yeah, he would give those babies more attention later. When his staff wasn't on the floor below listening to every moan. Not that it really mattered now. Folks on the other side of Main Street had probably heard his wife's scream of pleasure.

He softly pinched a nipple, and she gasped, "Easy." He gentled his touch even more and drew tight circles against her skin. It wasn't long before Carlie Beth's muscles started their familiar tightening around him.

He took her face in his hands, cradled it there and kissed her. He wanted to kiss these lips every day for the rest of his life. Would kiss them every day for a lifetime. "I love you," he whispered against her lips.

"I love you, too." Her orgasm pulled a long, luscious moan out of her as she ground against him.

Before she was completely finished, Grif pulled back and slid inside again with slow, deliberate strokes. He'd been primed since he'd put their overnight cases in the car, so it only took a few thrusts to send him over.

After, they were both panting and laughing softly. Grif pressed a kiss to Carlie Beth's naked shoulder and said, "You definitely know how to motivate a man."

"I figured you needed a little boost to finish the sandwich sign search."

"*I* needed it?" He laughed. "If I remember correctly, you got two boosts."

"Merely a sacrifice for the good of our hometown."

Reluctantly, he pulled out of her and gestured toward the bathroom. "I'll be on cleanup duty."

She smiled dreamily, and her eyes drifted closed. When he returned to the room, she was exactly as he'd left her. Panties around one ankle, bra twisted under her breasts, and a satisfied smile on her lips.

He stood in the middle of the room, letting the washcloth dangle at his side, and enjoyed the view. To think he might never have built a life with this woman. It gave him a physical pain in his heart. How easily could he have decided to stay in Los Angeles instead of returning to his hometown a few years ago.

Which would've meant a life without Carlie Beth. Without Aubrey and Stella Grace. At the ache in his chest, he pressed a hand there, the cloth wet and cool against his skin.

Carlie Beth finally opened her eyes and smiled. "What are you doing?"

"Thinking about what my life would've been like if I stayed in LA."

"Missing all the glitzy parties and fancy folks?"

He went to her and gently cleaned her. "No, thinking about all I would've missed here. What if I'd never known about Aubrey?" He knew Carlie Beth still felt regret for not telling him about their daughter years earlier. He was so thankful that Jonah had manipulated him into taking the city manager role in Steele Ridge. "The three of you are my life. My whole *life*."

"So you would've had another life."

"A piss poor one compared to what I have here."

Carlie Beth laughed and kissed him. "We both

got lucky when we found our way back to one another."

"Who could've guessed that one night in a Ford Taurus would be the best thing that ever happened to us?"

She hopped off the sill and reached for her clothes as if she hadn't felt sick a little while ago. "Then let's go find this sandwich sign so we can get back to all the great things we have planned for this weekend."

ONCE THEY WERE DRESSED AGAIN, CARLIE BETH WAS feeling so good, she could've run a marathon. Ginger ale, buttery popcorn, and sex would do that for a woman like her.

"Are you sure you're okay?" Grif asked her.

"Yep," she said, letting the cheer into her voice, "never better. So let's find this sign and get to Bryson City."

"Next on the list are crafters who might paint stuff like this, right?"

"I think Jennifer McKay is the only one who's done similar work."

"Then let's go find her."

Unfortunately, they discovered Jennifer was at a holiday market over in Statesville. So they headed for the interstate to the auto body shop. When they walked inside the gray corrugated metal building, Carlie Beth could smell the paint fumes even in the front office. She asked the manager if they could step back outside.

Grif got directly to the point of their visit. "Has anyone brought in the Mad Batter's sandwich sign for you to paint?"

"We don't really do work like that. Some motor-cycles and RVs, sure. Some custom car wraps, but no signs."

"Maybe one of the painters took on some side work?"

"I don't have a policy against it, so they usually tell me about their moonlight jobs. When would this have come in?"

"Some time last night. Maybe middle of the night."

"Lemme check." The manager went back inside and returned a few minutes later. "Nope. None of my people have seen it."

Grif shook the man's hand. "Thanks anyway." In the car, he turned to Carlie Beth. "I guess this means we'll have to drive east to Statesville."

Which would put them even farther away from their weekend destination, something neither of them wanted. "Let's think this through a little," she said.

"Isn't that what we've been doing?"

"Yes and no," she said. "You were convinced it was a prank. And then we figured someone might've taken it to restore it. Regardless, we've made some assumptions, but we've never stopped to ask who would benefit from the missing sign."

Grif groaned. "We have to run through the entire population of Steele Ridge, don't we?"

She patted him on the arm. "Don't be so dra-matic. Let's think about people and businesses with a direct connection to the Mad Batter first."

Grif leaned back against his seat and closed his eyes. "There was a rumor going around that El-maSue Smith's daughter was baking birthday cakes and selling them. Maybe she wants to take over the bakery business here in Steele Ridge."

"From what I heard about her red velvet, it would require more than a stolen sign for her to steal the Mad Batter's customers."

"Bad, huh?"

"Apparently she forgot the sugar a couple of times, and her cream cheese frosting looks more like cottage cheese."

"Okay, then maybe other businesses on Main Street wanted to divert foot traffic away from the bakery to their own businesses."

Carlie Beth took a scrap of paper out of her bag and jotted down several business names, including La Belle Style. "We haven't talked with Brynne. Why didn't we think of that first? She knows everything going on up and down Main Street."

"Maybe we could get away with just calling her."

"I doubt it since we'll likely be calling on other business owners."

Grif checked his watch. "Forty-five minutes. That's all we have left and then I'm declaring this a cold case."

Back in town, they entered La Belle Style with a cheerful tinkle of bells and found it full of holiday shoppers. Brynne had an upbeat violin version of a Christmas carol mashup playing over the speakers. The love seat near the front was piled with fluffy pillows that looked like snowflakes, and everything inside the shop was decorated with silver bows and glitter, perfect and girlie.

Girlie. Bows. *Shit.*

Carlie Beth leaned toward Grif. "Please tell me you bought wrapping paper and crap again this year."

"You make the cool stuff," he said, "and I make stuff look cool."

Thank goodness. Otherwise, the girls' gifts would be covered in newsprint.

Another panic-inducing thought struck her. "You didn't buy Aubrey her own car, did you?"

"Not yet," he sighed. "But you know it's coming."

She didn't want to think about it. Because that meant her baby—well, her older baby—would soon be flying the coop.

From behind the counter, Brynne waved at them. As always, her hair, makeup, and clothes were perfect. Some women were just like that. Carlie Beth wasn't one of them, but she was thankful to have a sister-in-law who would help her girl-glam it up on occasion.

They walked over, the hardwood floor creaking cheerfully underfoot, and Brynne asked them, "What are you two doing here? I thought you were going to Bryson City for the weekend."

"Long story," Carlie Beth said. "Have you heard anything about the Mad Batter's missing sign? Maybe some shop owner who's been jealous of their business or trying to steal customers?"

Brynne's red-painted lips tightened. "No. No way. That's not the way our small business council works. We support each other. If anyone was pulling that kind of crap, it wouldn't last for long because I'd kick their butts."

Carlie Beth looked up at Grif. "The one time we want people to be criminals."

"So I guess this means you haven't found it." Brynne snorted. "Don't tell Reid, or he'll be here in three minutes trying to horn in on the investigation."

"Why didn't I think of that?" Grif reached into his pocket for his phone, but Carlie Beth grabbed his arm.

"We still have thirty minutes. Don't give up yet." She said to Brynne, "We've been to the sign shop, out to the auto body place, and now here. We're missing something."

"Well, when there's a murder, the police always seem to look at those closest to the victim. Think that would apply here?"

The sign hadn't been murdered, but the bakery's business was being killed off without it. Who would benefit from that? Wait a minute... Who would benefit from a kidnapping rather than a murder?

Carlie Beth grabbed her husband and gave him a loud smack on the lips. "I know who stole the sign! This is a ransom situation."

"What? What are you talking about? Did we get a ransom demand that I missed?"

Carlie Beth tugged on his hand, pulling him toward the shop's door, and waved at her sister-in-law. "Bye, Brynne."

"Good luck!" she called out.

Outside on the sidewalk, she did a quick Google search and confirmed the address she was looking for. "We need to drive over to a house on Belvue."

7

As he'd done about twenty times in the past hour, Grif looked at his watch, and Carlie Beth said, "We have fifteen minutes left on the two hours you promised Camille, and I will have this thing nailed down in about seven."

"You're pretty sure of yourself."

She leaned in and gave him a smacking kiss. "Snagged you, didn't I? What's not to be sure about?"

Yeah, she could think that if she wanted, but he knew the truth. He'd been the one to snag her as the prize of his life. And she'd also given him two additional precious treasures. He could deny her nothing, so he drove to the address and pulled into a neat grass and stone driveway and up to a house that could've come off the pages of a fairy tale. Possibly if Hansel and Gretel's witch friend had been a sweet little old lady.

The yard was an immaculate spread of cool season fescue, and the sidewalk was lined with realistic-looking candy canes. "Do you think those taste like peppermint?" he asked Carlie Beth.

"It's entirely possible, knowing her."

"Her who?" He was trying not to give in to his impatience, but it was getting damn tough.

"Jeanine."

"I thought you said we were about to solve this thing."

"I said no such thing. I said *I* was about to solve it."

He pressed his lips to her hand as they strolled down Candy Cane Lane toward a white cottage trimmed out with the kind of decorations even Grif knew would make for a good spread in *Southern Living*. Fresh evergreen boughs were swagged along the wooden porch rails. Topiaries on either side of the door trimmed from more evergreen and poinsettias. Oh, yeah. If this place was good enough for *Southern Living,* it was good enough for *Steele Ridge Living*.

Bingo. Another economic development strategy. "We need a magazine."

"Um, I don't think pretending to be magazine salespeople will work," Carlie Beth said, staring up at him with a half smile on her face. "I'm fairly certain she'll recognize us."

"No, Steele Ridge needs a magazine. Something that will attract more tourists. An infusion of money."

"You don't think Jonah's cash is enough infusion?"

"The Baby Billionaire might have more money than he can spend in his lifetime, but the town has to quit relying on him to bankroll every initiative."

She cupped his cheek, gave it a light tap. "You've fronted the money for a few yourself."

Just like he would for this damn sign if they didn't find it soon. "Point taken. Let's finish one

Steele Ridge improvement project before we start another." He and Carlie Beth took the wooden steps to the front door that was decorated with a wreath made of sparkly fabric and teeny candy bars. "Stella Grace would lose her mind if she saw this. She'd think it was Halloween and want trick-or-treat."

"And whose fault is that? Maybe the man who taught her that flashing the Steele Shark smile with a flash of dimple would get her anything she wanted?"

Grif chuckled and knocked on the door. "She made twenty freaking dollars in cash that night."

"That's what a smile and those golden red curls do for a girl."

"If you want to smile and flash me your curls, I wouldn't say no."

Before Carlie Beth could give him a smartass comeback, the door opened, and Jeanine Jennings was smiling at them. She was eighty if she was a day and looked like a shorter version of the lady from the old TV show *Maude*. "Grif. Carlie Beth. What a pleasant surprise. I was just making some hot cocoa. Why don't you come inside for some?"

To Grif's everlasting frustration, Carlie Beth said, "That sounds wonderful."

No, it sounded like hell. Like sweet, polite hell. But he stepped inside that fairy-tale house anyway.

"Jeanine," Carlie Beth said as the other woman reached to help her off with her coat. "We won't be staying long. Just tell us where the bakery sign is and we won't bother you for any cocoa."

"It... well... it was taken."

"It sure was," Carlie Beth said cheerfully. "By you."

His wife was a smart one all right. They would get out of town soon.

"But... but I was the one who reported it."

"Of course you were." His wife gave Jeanine a sympathetic pat on the shoulder. "The whole sign-napping wouldn't have worked otherwise."

Jeanine's facade of innocence crumbled and her head drooped. "I was going to take it back." Her head came back up and her eyes were blazing with defiance. "You can't charge me with anything. It's *my* sign. It's not possible to steal something that's already yours."

It sort of was, but Grif wasn't going to get into felony theft and potential insurance fraud with the baker's assistant. "The Mad Batter lost a lot of business today. Isn't that stealing in a way?"

"I never meant..." She trailed off miserably.

Carlie Beth wrapped an arm around the older woman's shoulders and led her to a nearby chair. "Tell us about it. I promise we'll understand, and I bet Camille will, too."

"I wanted her to realize how valuable I am to the bakery."

"And you think she doesn't?"

"I asked to debut hot buttered rum cupcakes, but she said no."

Ah, so this was *actually* extortion. If this situation hadn't already taken two hours of his and Carlie Beth's getaway weekend, Grif might be impressed by Jeanine's thinking. As it was, he just wanted that fucking sign sitting back on Main Street. "And that's all you want," he asked, "to bake some cupcakes?"

Jeanine blinked up at him. "I wouldn't say no to a raise, but I promise that wasn't what this was about."

Grif had worked with Gordon Gekkos and Ebenezer Scrooges in his work as a sports agent. Jeanine wasn't any kind of negotiator or she'd have jumped on more money first. She just wanted to be appreciated, to be heard, to have some autonomy over her creative work. He'd be hard-pressed to condemn her for that. "What did you do with the sign? Did you destroy it?" Because if she had, he might have a harder time convincing Camille to listen to her.

She stared up at him, her mouth open wide. "What? No! It's in my mudroom by the back door. In perfect shape as always." She leaned forward as if to share a secret with Carlie Beth. "Did you know that sign was my mama's?"

To his everlasting disappointment, Carlie Beth dropped down on another chair as if settling in for story time. "Did she write things on it, too?"

"Five generations of Jennings women. Used to be, we kept it on the front porch, but then after Mama passed, I wondered why we should keep all that magic to ourselves. That's when I put it out in front of the bakery."

"Grif," Carlie Beth said, "in all the years back when Steele Ridge was Canyon Ridge and struggling economically, the bakery always did well. Sometimes I wondered if Camille was keeping it afloat with her own savings. But I bet you anything, she's turned a profit every year since Jeanine put that sign out in front."

In this town, just about anything was possible. Steele Ridge always had surprises up its sleeve. "Do you mind if I go in the mudroom and take a look?" he asked Jeanine.

"I guess I don't blame you for second-guessing me."

Sure enough, the sandwich sign was carefully folded and propped against the wall next to Jeanine's utility sink. Judging by the brushes and gold leaf paint sitting nearby, it looked as if she'd touched up the flourishes down the sides. The chalkboard had been recently cleaned, but Jeanine had already written a new message on it. *Life surprises you with gifts you didn't know you wanted.*

He returned to the living room. "It's here and looks better than ever." He pinned Jeanine with a serious look even though he knew she'd do whatever he asked of her. "I'll call Camille and make a special request from the city for a dozen hot buttered rum cupcakes, specifying we want *you* to make them."

Tears came to the older woman's eyes. "Oh, do you mean it?"

"Only if you promise to take that sign back to the bakery immediately and work ten hours for no pay. I figure you cost the bakery at least that much today." He smiled and reached to pull his wife out of her chair. "But I think she will have no problem increasing your pay afterward. Camille now knows exactly how valuable you and your sign are."

8

FINALLY. GRIF FINALLY OPENED THE CARVED-WOOD door to their suite. The champagne and strawberries he'd ordered were absent. Probably taken back to the kitchen for a cool down because of their late arrival.

So much for surprising Carlie Beth with a little romance. They tried their best at home, but romance was hard to come by with a teenager and a toddler in the house.

The room held a massive mahogany sleigh bed, a cozy sitting area with a stone fireplace, and big windows showcasing the mountains. But Carlie Beth only had eyes for the bed. She took one look at the massive mattress piled with goose down pillows, kicked off her shoes, and did a swan drive. All that investigation had apparently worn her smooth out. Within sixty seconds, she was curled into a cute little ball letting out a cute little snore every third breath. He pulled a throw—cashmere by the feel of it—off a nearby love seat and draped it over her.

His phone pinged with a text. It was from Maggie.

Heard Detective Parrish was on the ball today. Maybe I should offer Carlie Beth a job.

Grif snorted and thumbed in a reply. *It's Detective Steele these days. And if her snoring is any indication, blacksmithing is easier than I realized because this investigation business wrecked her.*

Maggie shot a response right back. *If you say so. Hope all your surprises this weekend are pleasant.*

Huh? Pleasant? If his cousin had been in on Carlie Beth's lingerie binge along with Tessa and Brynne, then she knew he planned for his weekend to be way more than *pleasant.*

He glanced at his still sleeping wife. She was crash city and would be for a while if he knew her.

It was fine. She'd have more energy when she finally woke. So he'd take this time to do even more prep work. If she wasn't wowed when she woke from her nap, he'd lost his edge.

And no matter what Reid said about Grif's minivan, he had *not* lost his edge.

He snuck out of the room and closed the door softly behind him. At the front desk, he stopped and asked the receptionist, "Can you point me to the nearest florist and jeweler?"

The young woman had waist-length pink ombré hair—he knew ombré because Aubrey had been begging it for it lately—smiled and said, "After you leave the property, go back to the highway. Once you're in town, take a left on Main and then another on River and I think you'll find what you need."

"Thanks."

When Grif's phone remained silent—no text from his wife—for thirty minutes, he knew he still had plenty of time. If Carlie slept for more than half an hour, she was in deep. And Grif sure as hell wouldn't wake her, because if she was roused during that intermediary hibernation, she was worse than a bear with acid reflux.

He returned to the room, his arms full of bags and boxes, to find his wife was still conked out. So he went to work on the room. No roses for his small-town girl. Carlie Beth liked sunflowers. The bigger, the better. And since it wasn't the season for them, he'd stuffed a florist's holiday stocking with a lot of bills for them. Although he'd hoped to take Carlie Beth out for a nice dinner after their first round of lovemaking, that plan was a bust. Good thing he'd already ordered something from the kitchen.

A quiet knock came at the door, and Grif opened it to a bellman with a skirted cart. "My wife is asleep, so I'll just take it in myself."

"Absolutely."

He handed the man a twenty for the privilege of having his wife to himself.

Ten minutes later, everything was perfect. Except that Carlie Beth was still dead to the world.

He could crawl up on that bed with her and wake her, but... yeah, he wanted his limbs to be stroked, not severed. A glass of Malbec in hand, he wandered into the luxurious bathroom complete with steam shower, gas fireplace, TV, and a jetted tub made specifically for two. He should probably turn the Kings-Timberwolves game on. He had a couple of clients playing, but damned if he wanted to watch sweaty men running up and down a court right now.

Instead, he ran a tub and dumped in some bubble stuff that smelled like vanilla and apples.

He was dozing in the water, in that twilight state,

when the bathroom door flew open. "You got me tacos!"

Carlie Beth stood in the doorway, a fish taco clutched to her breast like it was her firstborn. "Have you eaten?" she asked.

"Nope, I was waiting for you."

She made him smile with that lustful expression in her eyes. And it was all for the taco, not one iota of it for him. "I'll get you one."

She returned with the cart, rolled it straight into the bathroom.

"Dinner in the bathroom?"

"Grif, for what you paid for this place, I'm sure they clean everything three times."

He pressed the on button for the jets and said, "Why don't you wheel that over here and get in?"

"How hot is it?"

He'd refilled about twenty minutes ago, but he was a fan of the lava setting and Carlie Beth was more of a lukewarm girl. "Cool enough for you to put your feet in while you eat your taco."

"That sounds perfect." She dragged the room service cart along behind her. Unfortunately, she didn't strip all the way down, but she did drop her pants before sitting on the side of the tub and swinging her legs into the water. Fortunately, he was lucky enough to get another glimpse of the panties he'd stripped off her earlier.

And would again.

She passed him a carnitas taco and grabbed one for herself. Took a huge bite. It was one of the things he adored about her. She was no bigger than a minute, but she could put food away like a truck driver.

Carlie Beth swallowed and said, "These are

great. Maybe could use a little sriracha, but other-wise excellent."

Something about her comment tickled at Grif's brain, but he couldn't figure out what it was. "Glad you approve."

She leaned in as if to kiss him, giving him a nice view down her shirt. But instead of putting her lips on his, she took a bite of his taco.

"Hey!"

"I wanted you to understand how much I appreciate the gift of tacos."

"Understood, so hands off, Shortcake."

She took another bite of her own taco, then set it aside, which was an excellent sign that they were about to move from dinner to the evening's main entertainment. "I have a gift for you too," she said, standing to unbutton her shirt and drop it to the tile floor.

"I like it already." With perfect accuracy, Grif tossed his taco and watched it land on the cart. "Gimme."

"I'm a little afraid you won't like it."

Like it? Hadn't he already proved he was a superfan of the lingerie? "I don't think you have to worry about that."

He reached for her, but she turned away and picked up something off the tray. "Dry off your hands."

"Babe, they're just going to get wet—"

"Dry, or no gift."

Her no-nonsense tone sent an uneasy shimmer through him. He reached for the towel hanging on the rack to his right. "Done."

No teasing smile in sight, she passed him a large manila envelope. In fact, if he had to describe her expression, he'd call it worried. He didn't like worried, so he ripped the open the envelope flap.

"You might want to be careful with that." She sat back down on the edge of the tub.

He used more care to reach in and pull out a single sheet of heavy paper. It was black and white and looked like a reverse Rorschach test. Recognition landed in his gut and set off fireworks. Oh God, he'd seen one of these before.

He tried to toss it aside and reach for his wife, but she scooted away. "Look at it."

"I did," he said, catching her hand and lacing their fingers. "You're pregnant?"

She kicked her feet in the warm water and avoided his gaze. "I know this wasn't totally planned."

"Take off your underwear," he demanded.

"What?" She looked at him.

"Take off your damn clothes and come here."

While she did as he asked, releasing her breasts from her bra and lifting her legs to slide down her panties, he studied the sonogram a little more. Good thing he wasn't an obstetrician because these things just looked like a fuzzy TV screen to him. Whatever Carlie Beth wanted him to see wasn't happening, so he set aside the paper and took her hand to pull her over to straddle his legs. Sure enough, her belly was just slightly rounded.

He should've realized, but he'd been so damn busy with the holidays, Steele Ridge, and his remaining clients. "I'm sorry."

"Why?"

"I obviously haven't been paying you the attention you deserve if I didn't realize."

"I didn't realize until I started puking at around

two every afternoon."

Hands at her waist, he lifted her and pressed a soft kiss just below her belly button. "I don't care if it was planned or not. I love this baby already."

"Did you *really* look at the sonogram?"

"You know I can't make heads or tails of those things." He gently lowered her to his lap again.

She laughed and shook her head when his erection brushed her rounded little belly. "Well, the news didn't seem to cool you off at all."

"Why should it?" Grif lifted her breasts, kissed each tip. A woman's body was a true miracle. Bliss and birth all wrapped up in one. "I love you, Carlie Beth. The girls are going to be so excited, but for now, I want this news and you all to myself." He slid his hand between her legs to stroke the soft, slick skin there.

"There's more," she said, stilling his exploration with her serious tone.

The water suddenly felt as if it had dropped forty degrees, and he sat up until they were nose to nose. "Is there something wrong with the baby? It doesn't matter. I will love him or her, no matter what."

Carlie Beth cupped Grif's face and kissed one cheek, then another. "No, the doctor said everything is fine."

"Then what's the problem?"

"The problem is two heads."

"What?" A cinderblock took up residence in his chest. Jesus, this wasn't good, but they could— would—handle anything.

"You really need to learn to read a sonogram," she said. "There are two heads on that picture, because there are two babies."

He stared at her, mouth open until she nipped his bottom lip. "Nothing to say to that?"

"Uh..."

"That's pretty much what I said, too."

"Twins." The word just circled in his head like a bird with no place to land. "We're having twins."

"Yes, on or around June fifteenth."

They had a wonderful little family right now, but this... This was a kingdom. And he was officially the most procreative Steele of his generation. "I can't wait to tell my brothers and sisters."

"Because it's proof you have skills."

Now that the surprise was passing, Grif found he wanted his wife even more than he had before. She was giving him more babies. Two of them. "The person I most want to admire my *skills* is you."

She smiled and guided him inside her, taking him fully until they were chest to chest. "Oh," she sighed. "That feels nice. I'm glad you're not upset about this."

"Upset? Did you think I would be?"

"It wasn't planned."

"Most of the best things in life aren't." He wrapped his arms around her, surrounding her small body with his. Rocked up and against her until they were both shaking and moaning. She tightened and broke around him. Grif allowed himself to let go and gave himself to his wife.

Her head lolling on his shoulder, she said, "We might have to add on again."

"The house? No, we have plenty of room."

"I meant when it comes to cars." She grinned up at him. "I have a feeling we're gonna need a bigger minivan."

HIS HOLIDAY MIRACLE

STEELE RIDGE CHRISTMAS CAPER #3

ADRIENNE GIORDANO

1

S TUPID *FUCKING* LIAR.

Micki set the stick with its hateful little window and its even more hateful little two lines on the bathroom sink, then stared at it for a solid five seconds while reality set in.

Pregnant.

Knocked up.

How did this happen? She lifted her head and peered at herself in the mirror as panic exploded, searing her skin.

"Don't," she muttered.

In her lifetime, she'd faced her share of challenges. And panic didn't get a starring role in her coping-with-life strategy. But, dammit, she'd been so careful about never missing a pill.

Ever.

Except...

The ringworm. Or, more specifically, the ringworm medication.

A low moan filled her throat. *My God.* She still didn't know what she'd touched to catch that bit of nastiness, but the meds, her doctor had warned, reduced the effectiveness of her birth control. He'd also said the risk was low. Really low. She'd shared this with Gage, the absolute love of her life, and he'd seemed unfazed.

Then again, he was a man and when it came to sex, the big brain didn't necessarily do the thinking.

His swimmers—of course—defied the odds. Not a surprise, given she'd long ago nicknamed him Captain America or Mr. All-American or any other litany of names that put the most honorable man she'd ever met in a category he more than deserved.

She thought back over the last few weeks of brutal mood swings, touchy stomach, and...God, the fatigue. All of it made sense.

A knock sounded on the door and another spurt of panic ensued. Standing on the other side would be her blond-haired blue-eyed Iowa farm boy whose parents went to church—without fail—every Sunday. His family was about as apple pie as they came.

An unexpected pregnancy from Gage's reformed black hat girlfriend would put his mother in a straitjacket.

The knock came again. "You okay?"

Hardly. Definitely not okay. She glanced at the hateful stick again. Still two lines, still a positive result. Not that she'd expected it to change, but a girl could hope.

"Stupid, fucking stick," she muttered.

"Micki?"

If she didn't respond, Mr. All-American would knock down the door and rush in to save her. That's what he did. He saved people. Except, right now, she didn't need that. She needed to figure out how to tell him she'd colossally screwed up and—guess what, honey? We're having a baby. Lord, did he even want children?

They'd never specifically spoken of it, but he was most definitely a family man. Still, who knew?

She cleared her throat and pushed her shoulders back. "I'm good."

The doorknob turned and she snatched up the hateful pregnancy test, shoving it into her back pocket. She spun to face the door just as he poked his head through. His blue eyes that she loved from the moment she saw him zeroed in on her.

She forced a wobbly smile. "I'm almost ready."

Still with the intense eye contact, he tilted his head. "Babe, no offense, you look like hell. Are you sure you're up for this?"

The evening's festivities included heading into town for Steele Ridge's annual Novemberfest. The annual holiday festival was her brother Grif's brainchild and included a tree lighting and town merchants staying open late and offering big sales. As much as Micki hated crowds, she had to give her brother props on this one. Residents and tourists, cash and plastic at the ready, swarmed a closed-off Main Street.

Micki tugged on the hem of her Henley shirt while cursing herself for wearing such a formfitting garment. No way she'd walk by him. Gage, honorability notwithstanding, was after all a male. An extremely horny male who made little effort to avoid checking out Micki's rear whenever the chance presented itself. Today, he'd get way more than he bargained for with the test peeking out.

She leaned one hip on the sink. "I'm a little tired. That's all."

"Seems to me you've been a little tired for weeks

now. Maybe it's time to go to the doctor? Get some blood work done."

Blood work? Please. That's the last thing she needed. But right now, while confusion and life-altering circumstances loomed, the simplest thing to do would be to agree. Get her Mr. Fix-it sidetracked and off the topic of her health. "I'll do that. First thing Monday morning I'll call the doctor and make an appointment."

Technically it wasn't a lie. Given her current state of knocked-upness she needed to speak with Dr. Simons anyway. Figure out her options. As if there were any, because having her baby—Gage's baby—was the *only* option. At least to her. But what would he think?

"Good," he said. "Thank you. I'm worried about you."

This man. Always concerned about the people he loved. And even the people he didn't love. How many times had he stopped to help a stranger on the street simply because it was the right thing to do? How she, a hacker with a sketchy past, even deserved him she had no idea.

Maybe she didn't. Particularly after being irresponsible enough to get herself pregnant. Micki the screwup. No one should be shocked.

She pointed at the door. "I need another couple of minutes in here."

He nodded. "Sure. Take your time."

He closed the door and she stepped toward it, quietly flipping the lock before opening the under-sink cabinet and digging out the red toiletry bag Brynne had given her for her birthday. She tucked the test underneath the various compacts and mascara tubes.

Gage had seen her putting makeup on thousands of times and knew what the bag contained. He had no reason to rifle through it. And that made it the best damned hiding place she had until she figured out how to inform her man about his impending fatherhood.

GAGE HEADED DOWN THE STAIRS, THE OLD WOOD creaking under his feet. Normally, he didn't mind the sound. Micki had grown up in this house and the little reminders of its age made him think of his own childhood. Of his parents and family and a time when life was...well...easy.

Lately? Easy was scarce. Mainly because something was seriously off with Micki. For weeks she'd been dragging herself out of bed. A few times he'd come home from work early and found her curled up on the couch with a blanket for an afternoon nap. Micki? Not a napper.

At least not since he'd known her. And it didn't take a rocket scientist to know that when a person who didn't usually sleep a lot slept a lot, that person probably had a health issue. Thyroid maybe?

Or worse.

Cancer? MS? Addison's?

He stopped at the base of the stairs, took a look back. He hadn't heard her exit the john yet and it never took her this long to get her shit together. What the hell could she be doing in there?

Maybe he should take her to the ER. Micki's cousin Cash's girlfriend, Emmy, was an ER doc. She might be there and could do blood work. Figure out whatever this phantom disease was. Then, they'd make a plan on how to tackle it.

One thing was for sure: His girl was not herself.

The squeak of the bathroom door opening sounded. Finally. He peered up the stairs. "You good?"

"Listen Mr. All-American," she called, "knock it off. I'm fine. Just moving slow today."

At least her tendency to get testy when he went into fix-it mode hadn't been affected.

He blew out a hard breath and stepped away from the staircase. As much as it killed him, as much as this not knowing might eat him alive, absolutely rip him apart, he'd let her handle it. All he'd do is ask her on Monday if she'd called the doctor. That's it. She couldn't be pissed at him for caring. Even if she was, tough shit. He loved her.

He moved to the couch and dropped onto the arm to wait for her. That's all he could do right now.

A few minutes later her footsteps sounded above him, followed by the telltale creak of the steps. She appeared at the bottom, but instead of looking at him, she kept her back to him as she lifted her leather jacket off the wall hook. Then she bent low and grabbed her scarf and hat from the wicker bin on the floor.

When she finally turned to him, he studied her face. She'd slipped some shiny lipstick on and maybe added a little makeup, because her color was better. Not that pasty white from minutes ago.

He jerked his head. "Pretty lady."

That brought a smile to her face. Damn, he did love to see her smile.

"Handsome man."

He rose from the couch and met her near the door, holding his arms open for her to slide in for a hug. "Thanks for going with me."

She inched back, tipped her head up, and met his gaze. "Ditto. Besides, we can't miss Novemberfest. Not when it was our sort of unofficial first date."

It was way more than that. He'd never considered himself a romantic, but Novemberfest was special. Not only had it been their first outing together after they'd met, it marked the first time he'd ever kissed Micki Steele and now nearly three years later this had become a tradition. They'd return to the exact spot at the exact time and kiss. Just like the first time. Before that first kiss, he'd had no flipping idea Micki Steele would turn his life inside out. She'd changed everything and now he couldn't imagine a day—an hour—without her.

He loved her. Insanely. Her passion, her incredible drive to figure out how things worked and what made people tick. She did everything—including love—with ferocity. Hell, she'd run off to Vegas as a teenager and worked for a low-life, scumbag criminal to protect her twin brother. Did she even get what kind of strength that took?

He hoped to marry her one day. That, he knew, he'd have to tread carefully with. Loners didn't like people up in their business. Lucky for him he had patience.

A lot of it.

MAIN STREET WAS PACKED.

Jeez, Grif had probably broken the bank to advertise this sucker because Gage wasn't sure he'd ever seen this many people in their little town. Already, his skin started to itch. Since his traumatic brain injury, he'd stayed clear of busy places. Post TBI, loud areas rivaled an icy knife through his eye.

He and Micki stood near one of the barricades staring into the crush moving under a festive canopy of twinkling holiday lights suspended across the entire block. She glanced to her right where the side street blazed with blue and white lights for Chanukah and the entire downtown was an explosion of holiday cheer.

"My God," she said.

"Yeah. Between the two of us, this crowd is enough to get us committed."

At that, she laughed, but that extremely sweet sound was smothered by the squeal of a toddler—yikes, on that. Ignoring the said icy knife through the eye, he angled back, found the offending squealer and his parents not five feet away. Accompanying them was a teenaged boy moaning about the lameness of Novemberfest. These people had their hands full.

The couple moved around Gage and Micki and she let out a long sigh. "Kids," she said, giving him the side-eye. "They can be a challenge."

"Sure. That can be said about adults, too."

"True. Good point."

At the end of the block in front of the giant Christmas tree Grif had shipped in from some farm in the next county, the band did a decent job covering a Jason Aldean song. In his time here, Gage had expanded his musical library to include more country artists. Being from the Midwest, he'd been exposed to country, but it was his parents' country—George Jones, Hank Williams, Conway Twitty. This new country? He liked it. A lot. He also liked the way Micki teased him when he'd sing along in the truck.

The aroma of grilling meat drew his gaze left. He couldn't see beyond the cluster of bodies in front of him, but that smell came from the direction of the Triple B where Randi, the owner, and Britt Steele, Micki's brother and Randi's fiancé, were rumored to be manning a giant grill.

He grabbed Micki's hand and headed toward the B. "You hungry? I could eat."

"When can't you eat? I'm not ready, but you get something."

He refrained from telling her that, to his knowledge, all she'd eaten in the last six hours was a hunk of bread from the bakery.

"How about a snack?" he asked.

What ensued was one of those pain-in-the-ass sighs women did when they simply wanted to tell a guy to shut the fuck up. "I'll eat later," she said.

Of course. She was already rail thin and he didn't want her losing any more weight. Blood test. Definitely making her get a blood test.

"Hey guys," Randi said when they approached the makeshift snack bar.

"Hi." Micki stepped over to where Britt flipped a burger. She scooted to tiptoes and kissed him on the cheek. "Hey, big brother."

"Hey to you, little sister." He closed the lid on the grill. "Did you just get here?"

"We did. Gage is hungry."

Britt turned and reached to shake Gage's hand. "What can I get you? Burgers are almost ready."

"Give me a double cheeseburger. Extra cheese. Please."

"You got it. Give me two minutes." He jerked his chin right. "Micki, Evie is helping down at Brynne's shop."

"Ooh, I haven't seen her in three days." She wrapped her hand around Gage's jacket sleeve.

"Babe, while you're waiting on your burger, I'll run down and say hey to Evie and Brynne."

Evie owned and operated a med mobile. Basically a rolling doctor's office that serviced low-income areas. Given the recent flu season—a bad one at that—Micki's baby sister had been pulling double time.

Britt watched Micki head toward La Belle Style, the boutique owned by Brynne Steele, Britt and Micki's sister-in-law.

Once she was out of earshot, Britt jerked his thumb in Micki's direction. "What's wrong with my sister?"

Thank you. At least Gage wasn't paranoid. "Got me. She's been tired a lot. And moody as hell."

"PMS?"

"Hell if I know. And God knows I don't have the balls to ask *that* question."

"Smart man."

"I told her to make a doctor's appointment on Monday."

Britt lifted the grill cover and went to work adding cheese to a couple burgers. "I'll mention it to Evie. Maybe have her take a look at her."

Why Gage hadn't thought of that he had no idea. "Good idea. She's been this way for weeks now. It's not like her. "

"Maybe she's pregnant," Randi cracked from her spot at the portable register.

All movement seemed to stop—had someone just hit the pause button?—as Gage and Britt stared at her.

Micki? *Pregnant?* He thought about it. The sudden onset of fatigue, the sleeping—*a lot*—and the lack of eating. Just the other night she'd complained of a queasy stomach and nibbled on ginger snaps while he demolished a steak.

Could she...? Nah. He'd know.

Definitely. Plus, she'd tell him. He thought.

Well, shit.

2

———

MICKI WORMED THROUGH THE CLUSTERS OF pedestrians oohing and ahhing over crafty holiday wreaths hung on shop entrances and windows filled with fake snow. She'd like to get lost in this crowd. Or maybe slip into a time machine and go back... how long? Four weeks, six? Heck, she didn't even know how far along she was.

Damned ringworm.

Doing the math, she'd started the meds four weeks earlier. And then, two days ago, her period hadn't started. One day of total denial was all she'd needed before buying the stupid, *fucking* stick test.

A woman carrying a baby in one of those sling deals appeared in front of her, standing there for a few seconds, her gaze on Micki like this was some kind of weird message. Or, maybe Micki was just freaking out.

Freaking out.

Definitely.

Micki stepped aside, giving the woman as wide a berth as she could. As if somehow, even being near a baby would make her have twins. Or worse.

And, Lord, what a thought. She might have multiples inside her. *Too much thinking.* She took another step back, leaned against the cool brick separating the storefronts, and sucked in chilly evening air.

She'd never imagined this moment, never dared to. Spending the majority of her adult life distanced from family meant tackling problems and relationships on her own. Yes, she'd dated, even found a few really nice guys, but never anyone she'd hoped would stick around for the long run.

Never anyone she'd considered father material.

Most of the time she settled for companionship. Someone to talk to. The idea of children? Her? She had no doubt about her skills. Computers? Genius. Identifying weakness in others? Exceptional. Exploiting that weakness? Superb.

Motherhood?

Hell no.

Her life had been a series of bad luck, forced decisions, and fear. Always the fear. So much so that she never seriously considered—much less dreamed of—being a parent. Never mind finding the perfect soul mate to raise a child with.

Now, it seemed, she'd have both. Assuming Gage wanted it. In him she'd found the intimacy she'd craved along with a man strong enough to manage her aversion to that intimacy. Too many years alone had forced her to rebel against opening up to people. Any people. She was learning, though. And, if she did say so herself, she'd been a quick study.

Too much thinking. She walked another few yards and peered through the window of La Belle Style. Inside, her sister-in-law Brynne stood behind the desk chatting with a customer while handing over a large shopping bag. Along the far wall, baby sister Evie helped yet another woman by relieving her of an armful of clothing and carrying it to the checkout desk. The 'tis-the-season sale appeared to be working.

Brynne and Evie, two women she'd learned to confide in over everything from hand lotion to the best fitting underwear, stood just feet away. She trusted them.

But...a baby? That might be too much. Too personal, considering Gage didn't even know.

And suddenly going inside wasn't a great idea. Like Gage, these women had learned her moods. Blame all this learning to open up for that. Shame on her for allowing it to happen.

If she went inside, the way she was feeling right now, this confusion, this world-shattering mental battering, would tempt her to unload. And that would most definitely not be fair to Gage. If nothing else he deserved to know first.

She glanced down at her feet and the Chuck Taylor high-tops he'd given her. Her favorites that she'd paired with skinny jeans. Skinny jeans and sneakers, that was her. Soon she'd be ditching the skinny jeans. Were there maternity skinny jeans with a stretchy panel at the belly for her expanding midsection?

A flash of white appeared near the base of the brick lining the window. A bank envelope. The vertical ones folks stuck cash in. Someone must have dropped it. Thankful for the distraction of tossing away garbage, Micki bent low to pick it up. She wrapped her fingers around it and—whoa—was surprised by the thickness.

Was there actually money in it?

She stood tall, flipped the envelope over where

the flap had been loosened and pressed back into place. *Oh, no.* Someone had dropped their money.

She glanced around, looking for anyone rushing through the crowd or searching the ground. Nothing. Everyone went about their business, gushing over the upcoming tree lighting, bragging about the amazing deal they'd gotten on an antique sled or a cashmere sweater.

Whoever had dropped the envelope wasn't in her immediate area. And what if it didn't even have money in it? What else it could be, she hadn't a clue. She squeezed the envelope between her fingers. Had to be money.

Sliding her finger under the flap, she opened it and peeked inside at the stack of bills. She turned her back to the crowd and pulled the money halfway out, fanning through it. Hundreds along with twenties, tens and a five. Nearly eight hundred dollars.

Again, she stole a peek in all directions, but nothing. No panicked mom, no scrambling dad.

All right. Time for a game plan. Given where she'd found the envelope, reason dictated that, perhaps, someone had made a purchase, left the store and dropped the cash.

Brynne. She'd start there.

She entered the store, holding the door open for an exiting customer before heading to the register where Brynne finished ringing up a sale. Her sister-in-law handed over the purchase, thanking the woman.

Mariah Carey's jaunty version of "Santa Claus Is Comin' to Town" filled the store with holiday cheer.

Brynne cut her gaze to the approaching Micki.

"Hey there." She smiled, her whole face lighting up. "Evie," she called, "look who's here."

At that, Evie looked up from the sweaters she'd been showing a middle-aged man. Evie ripped off an excited smile. Her baby sister, always so happy to see her.

"Are you by yourself?" Brynne asked.

"Gage is down at the B getting food." Not wanting to waste time, she held out the envelope to Brynne. Keeping her voice low, she leaned in. "I found this in front of the store. Has anyone asked about a missing envelope?"

Brynne studied the envelope for a few seconds before meeting Micki's gaze. "No. Did you just find it?"

"Yes. Right outside." She leaned a bit closer, lowered her voice another notch. "There's roughly eight hundred in here."

"No way."

"Yes way."

Whether from her pregnancy or the thought of losing that much money, nausea flared. Micki held her breath a second, willing the sickness away before exhaling slowly. Air. Fresh air always helped, but she couldn't run from the store without causing a stir.

She refocused on finding the owner. "Someone must have dropped it out front. When they realize the money is gone, they'll retrace their steps and come looking for it. If anyone comes in and asks about it, give them my number. Don't tell them how much is in the envelope, though."

Brynne shook her head. "I won't. You should call Maggie. Let her know you found it in case someone calls the sheriff's office to report it missing."

Excellent idea. Micki retrieved her phone from her back pocket. Unfortunately, her cousin Maggie, Steele Ridge's sheriff, had left town. Micki and Gage had run into her earlier in the day when she'd been checking the placement of the street barricades before heading to New York to watch her stud football player boyfriend in a game.

Still, Maggie was never out of touch and Micki could at least alert her.

"She went to Jay's game," Micki said. "But I'll let her know in case she hears anything."

"Deputy Blaine was just in here. You might catch him outside."

"Will do." Micki turned back to Evie, who was still engaging with the customer. "Busy night tonight."

"It is. It's a great way to kick off the holiday shopping. I'll go relieve Evie so you can say hello."

"Don't bother her. I'll come back when Gage is done eating."

Just then Evie glanced over, giving her a narrow-eyed look that warned she better not be leaving. *Sorry, Sis.* Micki waved. "I'll stop back," she said, loudly enough for both Brynne and Evie to hear.

Right now she needed to call Maggie and hunt down Blaine — Deputy Do-Right, as her brother Reid called him—and find out who this envelope belonged to.

GAGE MADE GOOD USE OF HIS TIME BY WOLFING DOWN his burger while wandering toward La Belle Style. He'd managed to wave at a few folks without dropping his burger—or even losing one of the pickle slices he crammed onto it. Really, he should've ducked down the alley to the rear of Triple B where he could eat in peace, but...Micki.

He needed to put eyes on her. If for no other reason than to figure out if, in fact, she might be hiding something.

Something like a pregnancy. Which, holy shit, he couldn't get *that* out of his head.

He couldn't imagine it. Not the pregnant part— God knew they went at it like rabbits—but the secrecy part bugged him.

Don't. He couldn't get ahead of himself here. That never served. He'd wait and see how this played out. That's all.

Unless...

What if she didn't want a baby?

What if she didn't want *his* baby?

Nahhh. Come on? Sure, they'd never talked specifics, but he felt pretty solid that they were both in this for the long haul. But kids? Was that something she wanted? Damn. She'd never said it and he'd made assumptions he shouldn't be making.

Don't.

Ten feet in front of him, she stood beside the entrance to Brynne's boutique talking on her phone and dodging passing pedestrians. As he approached, she held her free hand up and if that pinched-nose look she wore was any indication, Micki was not happy.

Again.

Maybe he'd rethink his wait-and-see plan. From the time he'd met Micki, he'd played it straight with her. She'd spent the whole of her adult life employed and controlled by a slimy bastard—a fixer— who spared no expense to manipulate situations his way. It'd take years to undo the psychological damage that asshole had done.

Then again, they'd built their relationship on honesty. Micki demanded it. Accusing her of hiding a pregnancy? Total clusterfuck. One he wasn't willing to risk.

He angled around a thirty-something couple with a brood of kids. One, two, three...six. Wow. That was a lot of damn kids. Too many for him for sure. The young one, maybe three years old, let out a squeal that went through his brain like a pickax. He gritted his teeth until the brutal stab subsided.

Although he'd mostly healed from a TBI that had ended his military career, high-pitched noises nearly drove him to his knees. And young kids? Lots of high-pitched noises.

He eased up on the teeth grinding, forced his shoulders back, and let out a long breath. Concentrating on each area of his body—head, neck, shoulders, core—he visualized the tension working its way down, down, down, and sliding away. Between meditation and visualization techniques, he'd managed to control the stress—for the most part—that came with recovery.

Recovery was one thing. A secret baby? That was a whole other level. And, goddammit, how could she keep something like that from him?

Don't.

He shook it off, folded the foil wrapping down on his burger and, as good as it was, he couldn't finish it. Another thing to be pissed about. He stepped to the curb, tossed the sandwich into a trash can and kept his eye on Micki, who'd ended her call and was now texting someone. What the heck was she up to?

Intending to find out, he wormed through a group of teenagers and headed straight to Micki. "Hey," he said.

Giving up on her phone, she peered over at him. "Hi. You're not going to believe this."

In the time he'd spent around the Steele family one thing he'd learned was that when someone said something like that, it was usually a humdinger. And something told him she wasn't about to confess —in the middle of a packed Main Street—to being pregnant.

"Try me," he said.

She patted the front pocket of her leather jacket. The tip of what looked like a white envelope stuck out. "I found this. On the ground." She moved closer, then pointed to the sidewalk. "It has $765 in it."

Whoa. "No shit?"

"I think someone must've dropped it. I just called Maggie, but she's out of town. She said she'd let Blaine know in case anyone contacted them."

"Makes sense."

"I just tried Grif, too. Maggie said the festival keeps a lost and found and since Grif is running this shindig he'd know about it. Of course, my brother, being Mr. Busy, hasn't answered."

"It's nuts here. Give him a few minutes."

When she gave him a hard squint, he assumed he'd tripped one of her seriously touchy triggers. He cocked his head, stared right back at her, taking in her dark, chin-length hair that she used one of those dumbass straightening irons on every morning. The effect gave her an edgy, punk look that, twisted fucker that he was, got him hard. And, yep, his body followed his mind right over that cliff into XXX territory.

"Oh, my God," she said. "You're such a pig."

"What?"

"Please. You're thinking about doing me. I can tell."

He had to laugh. Had to. "Sorry. It's reflex."

She poked him in the chest. "This is a lot of money. Someone is probably in a panic and you're thinking about getting laid."

"Pretty much. Yeah. But, hey, it's lucky an honest person found it and will return it to the owner."

At the end of the block, the band fired up its version of "Jingle Bells" and Gage checked his watch. Almost time. "Let's head down and find our spot for the lighting."

She gawked at him. "How can you think about a tree lighting right now?"

Jeez. He couldn't stay out of the snake pit tonight. But, hell, was he supposed to ditch their whole plan when there was nothing they could do but wait? "Uh, maybe because the point of this is the tree lighting? And you've called Maggie and Grif. There's nothing else to do right now."

"Don't you care that someone lost their money?"

"Of course I care. You're doing everything possible. Watching the Christmas tree lighting won't slow you down. And why are you getting pissy with me?"

At that she rolled her eyes. Excellent. An eye roll. His mind wandered back a few minutes to Randi cracking that joke about a possible pregnancy. The hormones would explain her moodiness. He glanced down toward her belly hidden under her bulky leather jacket.

Micki typically favored formfitting clothes.

No.

What the hell was wrong with him? It was fifty fucking degrees out. She had a jacket on because it was cold. Besides, he saw her naked on the daily. He'd have noticed a baby bulge. For sure. No doubt.

Right?

He lifted his gaze, met her eyes again. "Are you sure you're okay? Because something is definitely up. If there's something going on, you can tell me. You know that, right?"

3

Oh, she couldn't tell him this.

No way.

She'd barely wrapped her mind around it, never mind bringing him into it. *Gee, honey, we've never talked babies, but you know, you must have some strong little swimmers because guess what? I was stupid enough not to take extra precautions against medication side effects and your Olympic-worthy sperm would not be denied.*

A couple pushing a double stroller with two toddlers in it passed them. Lord have mercy. By this time next year, they'd be parents.

Parents!

As much as she loved this man, as much as she knew—had total faith—that he'd protect her from any threat and support her through her worst screwups, somehow, she couldn't tell him.

Maybe that was selfish of her. To hang on to what they had today. Right now. Just the two of them. Happy and in love. *This* secret would change their lives forever. Hopefully in a good way, but she wasn't ready. Selfish or not, she *liked* their life. Liked waking up to quiet mornings and making love with no distractions.

Like a crying baby.

A hot, knifing panic built and swirled inside her, locking up her chest. What if he didn't want this? What if Micki Steele, the problem child, had torpedoed the one thing in her life that gave her total peace? With Gage came comfort and security and love. Total trust. Two people as close to perfect harmony as it got.

Was it too much to want to hold on to that? Did she deserve it?

Who knew?

But once she told him, everything would change. It would have to. There'd be three people in this relationship instead of two. And he'd have to go back to Iowa and explain to his straight-arrow parents they had a bastard grandchild.

Intellectually, she knew it wasn't fair to make a judgment like that. Gage's parents had always been kind to her. Even when their clean-cut, Mr. All-American son had walked into their home with an edgy hacker wearing mostly black and a skull ring.

"Micki?" Gage said, his voice a little sharper than usual.

His question. She hadn't answered it. Of course she hadn't. "I'm sorry."

"For what?"

For wrecking our perfect life.

The words were there. Ripe and ready on her tongue, but, no. Not here, not surrounded by all these people.

Besides, what if she hadn't screwed up? *Yes.* What if the test was wrong? Okay, now she might be reaching, but this sort of thing, she knew from Evie, happened all the time on various tests. False positives.

First thing Monday, she'd call her doctor. Get a blood test and be sure. The plan solidified itself, smothering her anxiety. She inhaled a soft breath and let it fly. She could do this. One step at a time.

She looked beyond him, to the couple with the stroller. Quiet. That's what she needed. "Can we go home?"

His head lopped forward and his mouth slid open. "Home? Now?"

The way he looked at her, one would think her head had fallen off and landed on his feet. "Yes. Now."

"What about the tree lighting? You know, our thing. The kiss at the exact time of our first kiss."

"I know, but..."

"But what?"

The snapping tone in his voice was an obvious indicator she was pissing him off. She couldn't blame him. Considering she was pissing herself off. "I'm just...tired."

So damned tired. Still, he deserved better. She inched closer, slid her arms around his waist and snuggled into him the way she always did when she couldn't get enough. Her safe place. Tucked right under his chin, inhaling his clean, soapy scent that made her feel like, despite their differences, two opposites really could make a life together.

When he drew her closer and set his hand on the back of her head, a little piece of her heart broke free. "I'm sorry," she said.

For so many things.

"It's all right. Nothing to be sorry for. If you're tired, you're tired. We'll go home."

. . .

THE SECOND THEY WALKED THROUGH THE FRONT DOOR
Micki silently hung her jacket on the peg, slid the
envelope from the pocket, and headed upstairs toward her office to see if she might be able to make
some progress on finding the owner of the envelope.

"You going to bed?" Gage asked from his spot at
the base of the stairs.

She paused on the sixth step and turned. How
many times had he chased her up the stairs, how
many times had they not even made it to the top
and wound up tearing each other's clothes off and
making love right here, on the staircase? Which
holy cow was not as much fun as it sounded because
it hurt her back something fierce. But his need for
her made up for all of it. He loved her. The catch of
the century and he wanted *her*.

Lucky girl.

She held up the envelope. "Grif hasn't gotten
back to me and there's been no word from Blaine. I
thought I'd do a little digging."

"Digging? I hope you're not thinking what I
think you are."

The man was no dummy; he knew her MO.
When she needed information, she got it the best
way she knew how. By hacking into any number of
databases. Illegal as it was, it was way faster than
waiting on people.

"The envelope came from Highland Bank and
Trust. There's a branch right here in Steele Ridge."

"Yeah and it's a fairly big bank. Branches all over
the place."

"But I can start with the Steele Ridge branch. If
someone knew about the Novemberfest deals, they

may have withdrawn the money today. It's a long shot, but you never know."

He folded his arms and stared at her. "You're gonna hack into the bank. I'm no lawyer, but I have to believe that's a federal offense."

Silly man. "Not if I don't get caught."

4

SATURDAY MORNING CAME WITH BRIGHT SUNSHINE, blue skies, and temperatures already soaring to a high of 68. This, Gage thought, would be a perfect day to take Micki into Asheville. Maybe grab some lunch or shop at some of those funky shoe stores she liked.

Anything to get her out of this weird goddamn funk. He hated this. Not so much the funk, everyone was entitled to that. What he hated was feeling shut out. From the start, they'd always been brutal with their honesty. She'd demanded it. Now? What the fuck? He was calling foul on her changing the rules without warning.

He rolled over in the giant king bed they'd bought together and found Micki's half decidedly empty. Another change in the routine. Typically on a Saturday morning he got up first so he could meditate, then grab coffee and check on the latest sports scores.

He rolled back over to check the time: 7:40. Yeah, way too early for his night owl and a spurt of frustration lit him up. He needed to know what the hell was going on. He threw the covers back, slipped on a pair of basketball shorts from the stack of laundry sitting in the basket on the floor. Eventually—like maybe next week—he'd get to putting it all away. Micki was better at that stuff than he was. The minute the laundry hit the bedroom she put hers away. Him? In good time. One of the many differences between them, but they still managed to love each other.

He wandered into the hallway and stopped. The bathroom door was wide open. No noise. *Not in there.* The clickety-clack of a keyboard tore into the silence. He walked to the middle bedroom they'd converted to an office. Micki sat at her desk with her back to him as her fingers flew across the keyboard.

"Good morning."

Her fingers still flying, she glanced over her shoulder. "Hi. Good morning."

"You're up early."

She went back to the oversized monitor. "I am. I couldn't sleep."

Another anomaly, since she typically slept like the dead. "How long have you been at it?"

"About an hour. Didn't have much luck with the bank last night and thought I'd try again. I'll get there."

And what was this obsession with this money?

A distraction, that's what. From whatever was bugging her. Randi's words from the night before slammed into him. *Maybe she's pregnant.*

He shook it off. Had to. The idea of Micki, the person he trusted above all others, hiding something like that? He couldn't go there.

"Or," he said, "since the bank is open on Saturday morning, how about we avoid you going to federal prison. Let's go there and tell them you

found the envelope. They'll look up any with-
drawals for that amount and maybe get a hit."

"I'm sure there are privacy laws. They won't
tell us."

"Maybe not, but if there was a withdrawal in the
neighborhood of $765 they might be able to call that
person and tell them you found their money."

Her fingers stilled on the keyboard. "Huh. I
didn't think of that."

Still staring at the back of her, Gage bit down to
release some negative energy. Damn, he needed his
morning mediation. "It might not work, but it sure
beats you sitting at the computer all day. Let's get
ready and head into town."

First, he'd meditate. Clear his mind and get centered for navigating this new world. Life with Micki.
The woman could be a challenge.

An hour later, they strolled into the bank where
two people waited between the rope lines for the
next available teller. Gage didn't recognize either
customer. Not that he knew every resident of Steele
Ridge, but a day didn't usually pass that he didn't
run into someone he knew in this town.

Beside him, Micki stared straight ahead, clearly
not interested in conversation. He resisted the urge
to ask her, for the hundredth time, if something was
wrong and the two of them stood in silence in the
old bank with its cracked marble floors and oiled
oak trim.

This had better work. That's all he could think.
If it did, Micki could put this obsession away and
maybe then she'd talk to him.

The three tellers all became available at the
same time. The two customers in front of them went
to the nearest windows so Micki and Gage walked to

the one on the end. Grace, a thirtyish blonde he knew from his many trips here, greeted them with a nod.

"May I help you?"

Gage hit her with his no-fail, info-getting smile. *You sure can, sweetheart.* "We were at Novemberfest last night and found a Highland Bank and Trust envelope with money in it. Appears someone may have dropped it."

"Oh no."

Micki leaned in, offering her own smile. "I feel awful about this. We've notified the police and town council, but we haven't heard anything. We're not sure the envelope came from this branch, but we were hoping you might be able to help us find the owner."

Grace cut her eyes to Gage and then back to Micki. "Hmm. Was there a deposit slip in the envelope?"

"No. Just the cash."

"I'm sorry. Without an account number, there's no way to know."

Losing her. "I understand." Gage upped the wattage on his smile. "However, it *is* an odd amount. We were wondering if you could look up if anyone withdrew the same amount."

"Ohhh," she said, her mouth forming a perfect circle. "I'm not sure I can do that."

Beside him, Micki cocked her head and narrowed her eyes. "You can't or you won't?"

Easy tiger. Gage set his hand on Micki's arm and gave it a gentle squeeze indicating she should shut. Her. Mouth. "No problem," he said. "There's probably privacy laws. How about we talk to your manager?"

Clearly relieved to shove them off, Grace bobbed her head. "Yes. She might be able to help you. Unfortunately she's off on Saturdays." She reached into a drawer and pulled out a business card. "Here's her name and number. You can call her on Monday morning. She's the only one with that kind of authority."

Damn. So much for this idea. And the way Micki was visually boring holes into Grace, Gage suspected it might be time to get her out of here before she went apeshit. God knew her mood swings were as unpredictable as the weather on Mount Everest.

"Really?" Micki said. "There's not *one* other person you can call to help us? An assistant manager? Something."

"Well, Marcy is the head teller and she's here." Grace turned to another woman counting out a drawer. "Marcy? Do you have a second?"

Micki peered up at Gage, gave him a sarcastic smile. "Now we're getting somewhere."

UNBELIEVABLE.

After being shut down—completely—by Marcy-without-a-soul, Micki stomped by Gage, who held the bank door open for her.

Dammit. These people. How could they not help? This could be someone's rent money and she was dealing with bureaucratic red tape bullshit. All they had to do was look at the amounts and see if anything matched.

"Don't lose your shit," Gage said in his ultra-calm and annoying I've-got-this voice.

She halted in the middle of the sidewalk, the

morning sun glaring down on her already heated cheeks.

"Well, good morning, you two."

Mrs. Royce, a mainstay—aka the town gossip—in Steele Ridge walked toward them with two women Micki didn't know. All of them more than likely were headed to the B for Mrs. Royce's typical Saturday breakfast.

Micki forced a smile. "Morning."

"Ma'am." Gage shot off one of his Iowa-farm-boy smiles and Mrs. Royce nearly cooed.

No cooing allowed. Not when Micki's head was about to blow off. And how about Gage being all cool and calm? She whirled on him. "Tell me that's not ridiculous. *Tell* me if ever there was a reason to lose my shit, this isn't it." She flapped her arms. "All they had to do was look!"

"They're rule-followers."

Ohmygod. Mr. All-American. *Totally killing me.* "Once in a while rule-followers need to have a *fucking* heart."

"My goodness!" Mrs. Royce said.

At her expertly dropped f-bomb, Gage let out a long sigh. He could sigh all he wanted. If things didn't start going her way, she'd be dropping a whole lot more f-bombs.

She headed back to Gage's SUV, her mind charging ahead to where she'd left off in her hacking efforts. She'd go back home and keep at it. With any luck, she'd get into the bank's files, find someone who'd made a withdrawal of around $765, and get their name and number. That's all.

Good plan. *Let's do it, sister.*

If, for some extraordinary reason, she couldn't figure it out she'd go back to the bank on Monday and refuse to leave until the manager did something.

Easy.

Peasy.

"Where you going?" Gage asked.

She stood at the passenger side door, her hand on the handle, waiting for him to unlock it. "Home. To figure out who this money belongs to. And I don't want to hear your objections. We tried it your way. Now we do it mine."

Just then her phone rang and she slipped it from her pocket. Brynne. "Hi, Brynne. What's up?"

"Are you still in town?"

"Yeah. How did you know?"

"I just got a call from my friend Marcy."

Marcy? Oh please, let it be the same Marcy. Might be time to clue Brynne in on her *friend*'s un-willingness to help.

"She works at the bank," Brynne continued, "she said you were just there."

Micki peered over at Gage, now standing on the curb, his head cocked as he listened. "We were. We're trying to figure out who this money belongs to and we're hitting dead ends everywhere. Marcy said she couldn't help us. *She* suggested we come back on Monday. Meanwhile whoever lost this money might be getting evicted."

From his spot on the curb, Gage sighed again. "Evicted? Really?"

"Yes," Micki told him. *"Really."*

And, Lord, she sounded like a crazy person. If this is what pregnancy did to her, she'd be a stone-cold psycho in a few months. Still, someone *could be* getting evicted and no one seemed to care.

"Micki," Brynne said. "Settle down. Marcy felt

bad, but all the tellers were watching so she had to toe the company line."

"The company line sucks."

"She feels the same way, which is why she called me. She went back to her computer and did a quick search."

Micki's shoulders flew back and she met Gage's eye. *Please, please, please let her have found something.* "Brynne, if you tell me she found who this money belongs to, I'll love you forever."

At that, Brynne laughed. "I'm hoping you'll love me forever anyway, but yes, she found something. You walked out so fast she wasn't able to get your number. So, knowing you're my sister-in-law she called me and gave me the guy's name."

"You have it?"

Finally, Gage stepped off the curb, heading straight for her. "What's happening?"

"I'll text it to you," Brynne said.

"Oh, my God, Brynne. Thank you. I don't want to go back into the bank and raise any suspicion, so please tell her thank you or send me her number and I'll tell her. "

"I'm heading down there to make a deposit. I'll tell her. Good luck. I hope this is the right person."

Micki disconnected, then bent at the waist propping her hands on her thighs and breathing out. A wave of nausea, whether from the baby or the adrenaline tearing up her system, assaulted her. She slowly inhaled and exhaled, repeating the process until her stomach settled down.

Gage's sneaker-clad feet came into view and then his hand was on her back, gently stroking and offering the comfort she'd come to rely on in so many ways.

"Babe," he said, "what's wrong? If you're sick..."

She straightened up and he immediately slid his arm over her shoulder, pulling her close. She rested her cheek against the soft fabric of his favorite Go Army sweatshirt and the frustration she'd felt minutes before slipped away. Gage did that to her. From the first day they'd met, he'd managed to help save her from herself.

"I'm fine." She patted his chest, then looked up at him. Her guy. To avoid being overheard by anyone within earshot, she went up on tiptoes, getting close to his ear. "Brynne is friends with Marcy. The teller. She looked in the system and found someone who withdrew the exact amount."

Her phone dinged and she stepped back to poke at the screen. "Ooh, this is it. Brynne sent me the name. We have to keep it on the down low, but it's something to check out."

Gage tilted his head to peek at the screen. "Brad Metzner. She even gave you his address."

"He lives in Hendersonville. Can we go there?"

"Yeah." He opened the car door for her. "We sure can."

5

Twenty minutes later, they climbed the three steps of Metzner's sagging front porch. Under Micki's feet, gray paint had worn through to bare wood. Years of traffic and the elements had not been kind to the exterior of the home, which only reinforced Micki's hope that she'd make a difference by returning the money.

If it did indeed belong to these folks. *Please let it be theirs.*

Gage gave the door a solid knock. He stepped back and—looking every inch the alpha male—squared his shoulders. Heat zipped straight from Micki's core. Whether it was hormonal overload or just her need to be close to the man she loved, she couldn't wait to get him home.

And naked.

The front door opened, snapping her from her naughty thoughts—dang that. A dark-haired guy, maybe late thirties, stood with his feet planted, gaze tracking from Gage to Micki and back. He wore ripped sweats and a paint-stained faded black T-shirt. "Help you?"

"Hello," Micki said. "Are you Brad?"

"Yeah. Who're you?"

"My name is Micki Steele. This is Gage Barber."

He lifted his hands palm up. "*Oh*-kay. Should that mean something?"

Fully understanding how crazy this must seem to him, Micki nodded. They could have been any number of scam artists coming to his door. And she knew all about scam artists. "This may sound weird, but were you at the Steele Ridge Novemberfest last night?"

Again, his gaze ping-ponged between them. Definitely freaking him out. However, she couldn't necessarily announce that she had found nearly $800 on the street and thought it belonged to him. She didn't know diddly about this man. If she gave him the opportunity, he could easily say the money was his.

If she gave him the opportunity.

Which she wouldn't do.

"Yeah," he said. "I was with my kids. And you better tell me what this is about before I call the cops."

Gage held up his hands. "Not necessary. We were at Novemberfest last night and Micki found something we believe might belong to you. Did you lose something?"

"Holy crap," he said, the words coming in an excited rush. "I sure did. My Christmas money. It was in an envelope. I went to the bank before the festival figuring I could start my shopping. My oldest daughter likes that pricey clothes store in town."

The pricey store had to be Brynne's boutique and since Micki found the envelope in front of La Belle Style...

"The envelope," Micki said. "Can you tell me how much was in there?"

"It was $765. Been saving it all year. Cleaned out all but a hundred bucks in the account. Did you find it?"

Micki reached into her back pocket where she'd tucked the money. She'd wanted it out of sight in case it didn't belong to Metzner.

She held the envelope out and her smile, for the first time all day, came easily. "It's your lucky day, Mr. Metzner. My sister-in-law owns La Belle Style. I think that's the clothing store you're talking about. I found the money on the ground in front."

He settled his gaze on Micki's hand, his lips parting, but not a sound coming through them.

"Dude," Gage finally said. "You all right?"

Brad ran both hands up and down his face, then held them over his mouth. "You have no idea how good I am right now. I was sick all night wondering what happened to that money. How the hell did you find me?"

"It wasn't easy," Gage said.

Micki nodded. "That's an understatement. We actually can't say. The person might get into trouble."

She handed over the money and he closed his hand around it. "I can't believe you did this. I thought it was gone forever." He paused for a second, shaking his head. "Wow. Just wow. I mean, who goes to all this trouble? Seriously, I didn't know what I was gonna do. I'm a single dad. My wife passed last year. Got four daughters and work two jobs to make up for my wife's lost income. This money? It's the difference between my kids having Christmas or not." He met Micki's eyes, his a little moist. "Thank you. You just made four girls very happy."

He stepped back and opened the door wider. "Please, come in. I got coffee on."

"No," Micki said. "That's not necessary. We just wanted to return the money." Then, on a whim, she dug her phone out. "And, I'll tell you what. I'll send you my number. When you're ready to go back to La Belle Style, text me and I'll let my sister-in-law know. Her name is Brynne and she's awesome. She'll help you pick out some nice things for your daughter."

Possibly at the Steele family discount.

"No kidding? That'd be great. What do I know about this stuff? My wife always did it. You people are something else. Real angels. You could've kept this money and now you're gonna help me shop? I'm...I don't know." He stopped, peered down, and cleared his throat before meeting her eyes again. "I'm blown away. Thank you."

And suddenly, Micki's heart shattered. Growing up, she'd always been the computer nerd. The girly girl stuff was reserved for Evie, but even shopping for jeans was always something Mom did with her girls. Brad Metzner's girls wouldn't experience that. Micki set her hand on her stomach and a vision of her baby—Gage's baby—filled her mind. Would she —or he—have blond hair like Gage's or dark like hers? What about his—or her—smile and eyes and laugh and every other possible thing inherited?

She wanted to see it. Every day experience her child growing and learning and just...being. Her eyes welled up, the punch to her chest so hard that she sucked in a breath. Focus. That's what she needed to do. Focus on sending Brad Metzner her number and avoid Gage seeing her fall apart.

She fired off a text to the number Brynne had sent her, blinked her eyes one, two, three times to clear the moisture, then held up her phone. "I just sent you my number."

"Hang on." He stepped away from the door for a few seconds and reappeared. "Got it. Thanks. My daughter said she put some things on a list at the store, but I'll definitely take you up on the help."

"Absolutely," Micki said. "Happy to do it." Hoping she'd pulled herself together enough, she peered up at Gage. "Are you ready? I think we've completed our mission."

For the first time in his life, Gage finally understood what people meant by deafening silence. He'd always been a skeptic of that particular phrase. What the hell did that even mean? Silence being deafening. It made no sense.

Until now.

The entire ride home Micki had stared out the window, her mouth decidedly shut. Not a peep or even a glance over at him. Being more of a loner, she was never one for gratuitous conversation or fits of excitement. But, hell, she'd done exactly what she'd set out to and made a stranger's life a whole lot easier. It should have warranted *something*.

He pulled into their driveway, parked, and killed the ignition. The second she reached for the door handle he blurted, "I don't get it."

She climbed out of the truck and swung back to him, her face pasty white and filled with misery. What the fuck? How could she be miserable right now?

"What?" she asked.

"Why are you so damn moody? You wanted to find this guy. We found him. You didn't say two words the whole ride home."

"I'm not *moody*. The man's wife died. I'm supposed to celebrate that?"

Now she wanted to spin this thing? Nuh-uh. *Sorry, babe.* She whipped the door shut and headed for the house. Hopping from his seat, he hit the lock button and strode after her. "That's not what I'm talking about and you know it. For weeks I've been asking what's going on. You haven't been yourself. Now I want answers. Are you unhappy? Is it me?"

"Oh my God."

She unlocked the front door and rushed inside, once again not bothering to fucking look at him. Damn, this woman frustrated him sometimes.

"Micki!"

Once inside, he pushed the door closed—no sense letting the neighbors in on their fight. He and Micki didn't go at it all that much, but when they did, it got loud. And if he were a betting man, he'd bet they were about to have a total blowout.

He stood at the base of the steps while she paced the length of the living room, reached the edge of the sofa, then turned for another lap. At least she wasn't running from him, trying to avoid the conversation.

That alone felt like progress, so he eased out a breath, focused on relaxing his shoulders. His meditation practice, something he'd come to rely on heavily after his TBI, had taught him the value of a time-out. Even a few seconds of quiet calmed his nerves and centered him.

"Are you going to talk to me?"

She completed another lap, sparing him a quick

glance when she reached the front wall. "I'm terrified."

"Of what?"

"Everything."

Ha. As if that narrowed it down? How the hell did they get to this point? A few weeks ago, their relationship seemed rock solid. At least he thought... "Everything? What does that mean? And, for God's sake, stop pacing. You're giving me vertigo."

At that, she halted. Having lived with him, she knew brain injuries were a tricky thing. Vertigo? It happened sometimes. "Thank you," he said.

Across the room, she met his gaze and something in her haunting eyes—the ones he loved to stare into all night—broke him. *How did we get here?* He moved toward her, stopping a good two feet away. When upset, Micki liked her space. "Micki, please. Talk to me. Let me help you."

And then—oh shit—her eyes welled up. Micki. Crying. God help him, if she told him she'd gotten busted hacking and was going to prison, he'd lose his mind.

"You," she said, "are the best thing that has ever happened to me. Before you, I was alone and...misunderstood. If you hadn't come into my life I would've run away from here. I would've left my family forever."

A fierce clanging hammered at his ears. He did *not* like the sound of this. Had her past caught up with her? The scumbag from Vegas?

He stepped closer, held out his hands. "Whatever it is, you know me, we'll work it out together. The way we always do."

"I know. But, you won't be happy."

. . .

THE JIG WAS UP. SHE HAD TO TELL HIM. HAD TO. Hiding it wasn't fair to him and it was tearing her up, which wasn't good for the baby.

Their baby.

She reached for his still extended hands and squeezed. "We have a problem."

"I figured. Are you in trouble? Or sick?"

"No."

He let out a long breath, his shoulders dipping with relief. Poor Gage — Captain America — some things even he couldn't fix.

"Good. Anything else, we can fix. Believe me."

They'd see about that. "I'm glad you feel that way because, well, I have an unexpected surprise."

"Micki, please, before I have a fucking stroke just tell me what's wrong."

She bobbed her head, forced her mouth open. *Tell him.* Let it go. "I'm…"

"What? Spit it out."

The word was stuck. Glued to her tongue because what if…

Forget that. What-ifs didn't matter now. She needed to face this. And maybe, just maybe, telling him would relieve the pressure. Let her think clearly. He did that for her. Helped her concentrate on the important things.

"I'm pregnant."

6

HIS HEAD DIPPED FORWARD, BUT HIS FEATURES remained neutral. No raised eyebrows or grimacing. Or swearing even. Must've been the shock rendering him speechless.

"I'm so sorry," she said her voice cracking with the effort. "I promise you, I didn't do it on purpose. I've been taking my pills. The only thing I can think is that I started taking that ringworm medication and it counteracted my pill. I don't know."

His mouth opened and hung for a second until he blinked, then blinked again. "Preg—how long have you known this?"

"I found out last night. That's what I was doing in the bathroom when you knocked on the door. I'd just taken the test. It was one of those pee-on-the-stick things."

He dropped his chin to his chest, forced out a hard breath. "Okay. Good."

"Good?"

He lifted his head, met her eyes. "You haven't been keeping it from me."

"No. I wanted to tell you. I was," she flapped her arms, "scared, I guess."

"Of me?"

"No. Never."

Squeezing her hands, he cocked his head. "Then what?"

How to admit it? That she'd failed him by letting this happen. By fast-tracking their relationship with a child. "Of disappointing you. We've talked about the future, but not like this. In all our conversations nothing ever came up about us having a baby so soon. Or at all."

"That's true, but, you know, we're not stupid people. When you have sex, sometimes a baby happens."

Gage. How she loved him. The man was a master at relieving burdens. "Well, sure, but your parents. I don't think they'll approve and then I'll be the witch who trapped their son."

He stepped back, literally, as if he'd been slugged.

She was blowing this. Big time. "Wait. No. That came out wrong. Your parents are great. I know that. But I also know I'm not necessarily what they pictured for you. Somehow I think they'd prefer a blond, church-going lawyer or doctor versus a skull-wearing hacker."

He continued to stare at her. Silence and tension built, climbing higher and higher and her blood whooshed, making her ears ring. His hands moved and she cut her gaze to them. *Letting go.* She squeezed, as if that would keep him from pulling away from her. But, no. Inch by tiny inch, which somehow made this all the worse, he freed his hands from hers.

"Gage, please—"

"First of all, you have no idea what my parents

think or don't think. They've never said one even semi-negative thing about you. You make me happy and that makes them happy. That's all they care about."

"But this is different. This is a baby. A bastard grandchild."

SHE DID *NOT* JUST USE THAT WORD TO DESCRIBE HIS child.

Gage clamped his jaw shut, ground his teeth so hard they throbbed. Relax. *Deep breath*. He'd need a month of meditation after this. Inhaling, he counted to three, then let it go.

Not only had she not clued him in to her suspicions about being pregnant—logically, he could get around that because knowing her, she'd want to be sure. But she'd made assumptions—really shitty ones—about his parents. And that completely pissed him off.

For months, he'd been dealing with Steele family drama, never complaining, never rocking the boat, and always supporting her. No matter what those fuckers had going on, he'd hung in there. Stayed positive.

"Don't," he said, his voice low and so tight it might asphyxiate him, "ever use that word to describe our baby. What is this? The 1950s? Yes, my parents have deep faith, but I know them. If we're happy, they'll be happy and they'll love our baby because it's mine. Because they love *us*. Would they prefer us being married first? Probably. But not because of some ancient thinking about babies out of wedlock. They'd want us to have a plan. That's all. No surprises. This? Yeah, it's a surprise."

"I'll say."

"And, maybe it's not the timeframe I'd have preferred, but it is what it is. Nothing will change that, so we might as well be happy about it."

"Are you? Happy about it?"

"Are you? Aside from the initial shock and being afraid to tell me? Do you want my baby?"

She nodded. "Yes. You're *everything* to me. After talking to Brad Metzner today and hearing about his wife, I knew for sure I wanted our baby. I'll love him —or her–even more because he's ours. I was just terrified you'd hate me for it."

"After everything we've been through, how could you think that?"

She shrugged. "I don't know. I panicked. I was worried you didn't want kids. And the more I went down that rabbit hole, the worse it got."

"Just because we hadn't talked about it, doesn't mean I don't want kids." He ran one hand over his face. "A baby. Wow."

"It's sinking in, right? That's how I felt last night. A little dazed, my emotions all jumbled up inside. If you need to take a minute to think it through, that's fine."

He reached for her hands again and squeezed. "I don't need a minute. I don't need any time at all. I love you. We're having a baby. What's to think about?"

She shrugged. "Are we ready to be parents?"

He laughed. "Is anybody ever ready? We'll figure it out as we go along. Like everyone else."

How did she, Micki Screwup Steele, get so lucky as to find this guy? "You know people around here will gossip."

"No doubt. They gossip about everything. Someone steps on gum and they chatter about it. And if the old farts wanna judge us, let them. Between all of your relatives, that'll get straightened out real quick."

Now that would be fun. One thing about the Steele gang, they stuck together. "That's true."

"Stop worrying about everyone else. Forget them. This is you and me. And we're having a baby." He smiled. "We're gonna be a mom and dad. How cool is that?"

A SPURT OF EXCITEMENT AND RELIEF—ALL WARM AND bright and happy—exploded inside Micki.

She yanked her hands free of Gage's grasp and threw her arms around his neck, kissing him hard on the mouth.

How she loved this man.

Once again, he'd freed her from herself. Instead of judging her and being angry and storming out, he'd done what he'd always done.

He'd *stayed.*

"I love you," she said. "You have no idea. There is no one—not one man—I could ever see having a baby with other than you. You're patient and reasonable and, and...kind. Just amazing."

He flashed a smile that rivaled the Main Street holiday lights. "Well, let's not get crazy."

Too bad, hotshot. "Oh, I'm getting crazy. Believe me." She smacked another kiss on him. "Really crazy."

"I *love* you," he said. "Whatever goes on with you —with us—we're a team. Always. There is *nothing* you can't tell me. I mean, yeah, some things, I might not like, but I'll always listen. And I'll always help you figure it out. Got it?"

How, after everything she knew about him, could she have forgotten? She jerked her head. "Got it."

"Good. Now, we have a bigger issue."

Bigger than an unplanned pregnancy? This should be good. "Uh, really?"

"Uh," he mimicked. "Yeah. And it's big."

"What's bigger than an unplanned pregnancy?"

"How about who we tell first? Your folks or mine?"

Micki took that in. Her family, simply based on proximity, typically heard things first. Half the time, the gossip mill took care of it for them. This time, they'd contain it. Make sure it came from them directly.

But Gage's parents, simply based on geography, never got first crack at news regarding their son. And that just didn't seem fair.

"Yours," she said. "After all of this, the doubts I had about their reaction, they deserve to hear it first. Plus, it's the holidays and you don't get to spend much time with them. I think we need a road trip."

His eyebrows hitched nearly to his hairline. "To *Iowa*?"

She grinned. "It'll give us time alone. To plan. And think about—"

"Baby names."

Whoa, big fella. Easy, now. "Holy cow, Gage. I wasn't thinking that just yet, but...well, sure. Okay. Baby names and ultrasounds and whether we want to know the sex and whatever else we can think of. So, what do you think, Captain America? Should we go to Iowa and tell your parents our news?"

He reached for her, pulling her close and squeezing her against him. Her favorite spot. Right here, with Gage.

He patted that spot on her lower back that automatically drew his attention and she let out an easy sigh. Before Gage, she'd never experienced the normalcy of a man touching her in a familiar way.

Another thing she'd always cherish.

"Yeah," he said. "I think we should. I love you, Micki Steele. You make me nuts sometimes, but I love you. Always will. We're building a life together."

And that was all she could ask for.

———

Read on to enjoy an excerpt of A Holly Jolly Homecoming, Steele Ridge Christmas Caper #4.

A HOLLY JOLLY HOMECOMING

BY TRACEY DEVLYN

SEVENTY-ONE, SEVENTY-TWO, SEVENTY-THREE...

Coen Monroe pushed up, trying like hell to keep pace with the maniac beside him, ignoring the burn in his biceps. Now that the holidays were closing in, someone at the training center had decided to swap out their workout jams with cheery Christmas music.

Cheery didn't feed his adrenaline. Bass. He needed a lot of bass.

"Grandma got run over by a reindeer..."

He closed his eyes and tried like hell to block out the violent reindeer. The darkness only seemed to amplify the volume.

"How long is your leave?" Reid Steele asked around a hard breath.

Sweat dripped from Coen's nose onto the mat beneath him. "I head back to base the day after Christmas."

"Riley coming home?"

His eyes lost focus, burned. "No."

"You going there?"

There. Virunga Massif. A natural wonder in the

heart of Africa, containing three national parks and eight volcanoes. All just a grenade throw away from some of the most vicious fighting and crimes against humanity in the world. Some referred to the civil unrest as the Third World War.

Most knew nothing of the region's conflict and those who did had no clue how to put an end to it.

But Riley knew all about it, and she'd spent most of the last eighteen months in the thick of it all.

"No." Behind him, Way Kingston set a pounding pace on his treadmill. Coen increased his rhythm to match Riley's brother's running steps.

One-seventeen, one-eighteen…

He drove himself harder, faster. Reached for the next push-up and the next and the next.

One thing was for sure, he'd keel over before allowing a sissy-ass Green Beret to out-push him.

"Something. Going. On?" Reid's clipped question revealed he was suffering as much as Coen.

"Schedule conflict." He was grateful their workout prohibited in-depth explanations, because he had none.

He'd known a lengthy separation from Riley would be tough, but he'd underestimated how difficult it would be. It was nothing like leaving a friend or parent or sibling. The love he had for her was bone-deep, aching, almost debilitating in its demand for constant connection. He needed the warmth of her hand in his, the fresh Carolina air weaving through her hair, the soft unbreakable bond of her lips against his.

During the first few months of their separation, he'd been busy reacclimating to military life at Fort Bragg and getting briefed on current, international hot spots. He'd managed to separate his personal life from his professional one—until Riley's plane set down in the Democratic Republic of Congo four weeks later.

From that point forward, she'd consumed his thoughts. Every day, every hour. Every damned minute.

Was she safe? Happy? Still terrified of failing? How was her research going? Had she made friends?

Were any of them guys?

Was her love for him fading?

Their weekly video chats answered some of his questions. But the others, the ones that could shatter him, remained unasked and unanswered.

"Had enough, Sarge?" Reid panted.

His arms shook and his gut cramped, but he refused to break pace with the man next to him. Refused to consider that Riley could live without him—

He shook his head. Focus, Monroe. Push-ups. "I got ten more in me," he gritted out. "You?"

Reid lasted for another three before falling into a heap of sweat and exhaustion.

He dug in for seven more before his knees hit the mat. He sat back on his haunches, wondering if his victory would be interrupted by a bout of puking.

A long, low whistle pierced through their harsh breaths.

"Way to kick ass, boys." Gage Barber shut the door to the small refrigerator in the back of the weight room. "One hundred and forty-five in two minutes is a record for the center." He tossed a water bottle to Coen. "Delta Force really are badasses." At

Reid's look of where's-my-water, Gage shrugged. "Last one."

"Did you doubt it?" Coen broke the cap seal and handed the bottle to Reid.

"Humble." Reid dragged himself up onto one elbow and downed half the water before handing it back to Coen. "Thanks."

"Not me, but your partner there," Gage nodded toward Reid, "seemed to believe a ten-year-old could beat you."

Unrepentant, Reid jiggled his eyebrows.

Coen swiped a dribble of water from his chin. "He shouldn't hold everyone to the same bar as himself."

"Jagoff."

"Pansy ass."

"High-school regression again?" A slender hand snaked around Gage's middle seconds before a dark-haired beauty, sporting black thick-soled boots and leather jacket and a white scarf dotted with tiny, red skulls and crossbones appeared on the former Green Beret's opposite side.

A slow smile raked across Gage's all-American face as he angled around to draw Mikala Steele into his arms. He kissed her temple.

"So says the skulls-wearing Goth," Reid said before lobbing Coen's empty water bottle at his sister's head.

Gage caught it in midair, earning him a grateful lick-kiss to the neck.

Reid made a hacking noise in the back of his throat. "Spare me from the public display of neck-licking, would you?"

Micki smirked at her brother.

Coen got to his feet and held out a hand to his friend. "Nice workout, old man."

Clasping Coen's hand, Reid rose in one smooth motion. "Next time, I'll forgo the breakfast burrito."

Way slowed his full-out run to a jog.

"What brings you here?" Gage asked Micki.

"Mom sent me."

Reid groaned. Gage leveled a you're-screwed look on Coen. Micki smiled.

"What?" Coen asked.

"Run while you can," Reid said.

Unease slithered through his chest. "Spew it."

"The city is organizing a Christmas potluck," Micki said. "Mom—and Aunt Sandy—would like all of us to be there." She patted Gage's chest in what some women would call a comforting gesture. But with Micki, it had more of a suck-it-up vibe.

"I've never known the two of you to turn down a free meal," Coen said. "What's the catch?"

"The potluck is bait," Reid said.

"For what?"

"To get reluctant servicemembers to show," Micki said.

"Why would they be reluctant?"

"The city wants to honor us." Gage scrubbed the back of his neck. "All of us. Active and veterans."

All the muscles in Coen's back contracted. "Is Grif pushing this?"

Way slowed the treadmill to a walk.

"No," Reid said. "Though he's not opposed to it. But he knows how we feel about pomp and shit."

"I might need to go visit my family in Bryson City a few days early," Coen said.

"There's no pomp and shit." Micki sent her

brother a shut-it glare. "We'll eat. They'll read your names. Everyone claps. Nighty-night."

Riley would know how to get him out of this.

If she were here.

But she wasn't.

Check out the Steele Ridge website for information on all of our Christmas Capers.

DISCOVER MORE STEELE RIDGE

STEELE RIDGE CHRISTMAS CAPERS

STEELE RIDGE: THE STEELES

STEELE RIDGE: THE KINGSTONS

ALSO BY TRACEY DEVLYN

NEXUS SERIES

Historical romantic suspense

A Lady's Revenge

Checkmate, My Lord

A Lady's Secret Weapon

Latymer

Shev

BONES & GEMSTONES SERIES

Historical romantic mystery

Night Storm

TEA TIME SHORTS & NOVELLAS

Sweet historical romance

His Secret Desire

ALSO BY KELSEY BROWNING

PROPHECY OF LOVE SERIES

Sexy contemporary romance

Stay With Me

Hard to Love

TEXAS NIGHTS SERIES

Sexy contemporary romance

Personal Assets

Running the Red Light

Problems in Paradise

Designed for Love

SEASONED SOUTHERN SLEUTHS MYSTERY SERIES w/NANCY NAIGLE

Southern cozy mysteries

In For a Penny

Collard Greens and Catfishing

Deviled Eggs and Deception

Fried Pickles and a Funeral

Wedding Mints and Witnesses

JENNY & TEAGUE NOVELLAS

Contemporary romance with a dab of mystery

Christmas Cookies and a Confession

Sweet Tea and Second Chances

NOVELLAS

Sexy contemporary romance

Amazed by You

Love So Sweet

ALSO BY ADRIENNE GIORDANO

THE LUCIE RIZZO MYSTERY SERIES

Dog Collar Crime

Knocked Off

Limbo (novella)

Boosted

Whacked

Cooked

Incognito

Romantic suspense books available by Adrienne Giordano

PRIVATE PROTECTOR SERIES

Risking Trust

Man Law

Negotiating Point

A Just Deception

Relentless Pursuit

HARLEQUIN INTRIGUES

The Prosecutor

The Defender

The Marshal

The Detective

The Rebel

JUSTIFIABLE CAUSE SERIES

The Chase

The Evasion

The Capture

CASINO FORTUNA SERIES

Deadly Odds

JUSTICE SERIES w/MISTY EVANS

Stealing Justice

Cheating Justice

Holiday Justice

Exposing Justice

Undercover Justice

Protecting Justice

Missing Justice

Defending Justice

SCHOCK SISTERS MYSTERY SERIES w/MISTY EVANS

1st Shock

2nd Strike

3rd Tango

ABOUT TRACEY DEVLYN

 *USA Today* bestselling author **Tracey Devlyn** wanted to be the next Dian Fossey and explore the wilds of Africa, but that was before she met chemistry and calculus and realized a business major, rather than a science degree, might be a better fit. With an enthusiasm for research that translates into creative (and disturbing) plot twists for her characters to navigate, it's no surprise that her suspense-laden stories excite her readers and offer a glimpse of the nefarious nature lurking behind her sweet smile. Despite the thrilling, emotional ride she gives her readers, Tracey enjoys an annoyingly normal lifestyle with her husband and rescue dogs at her home in the mountains of North Carolina.

Don't miss a new release! Join Tracey's New Release Newsletter list at https://TraceyDevlyn.com/Contact!

For more information on Tracey, including her Internet haunts, contest updates, and details on her upcoming novels, please visit her at:
www.TraceyDevlyn.com
tracey@traceydevlyn.com

ABOUT KELSEY BROWNING

 *USA Today* bestselling author **Kelsey Browning** writes contemporary romance, romantic suspense, and cozy mystery. Originally from a Texas town smaller than the ones she writes about, Kelsey has also lived in the Middle East and Los Angeles, proving she's either adventurous or downright nuts. These days, she makes her home in northeast Georgia with her tech-savvy husband, her smart-talking son, and a (fingers crossed) future therapy pup. Find Kelsey online at KelseyBrowning.com.

Kelsey can be found on:
    www.KelseyBrowning.com
    Facebook.com/KelseyBrowningAuthor
    instagram.com/kelseybrowningauthor
    Pinterest.com/KelseyBrowning
    Goodreads.com/KelseyBrowning

ABOUT ADRIENNE GIORDANO

 **Adrienne Giordano** is a *USA Today* bestselling author of over forty romantic suspense and mystery novels. She is a Jersey girl at heart, but now lives in the Midwest with her ultimate supporter of a husband, sports-obsessed son and Elliot, a snuggle-happy rescue. Having grown up near the ocean, Adrienne enjoys paddleboarding, a nice float in a kayak and lounging on the beach with a good book. For more information on Adrienne's books, please visit www.AdrienneGiordano.com. Adrienne can also be found on Facebook at http://www.facebook.com/AdrienneGiordanoAuthor, Twitter at http://twitter.com/AdriennGiordano and Goodreads at http://www.goodreads.com/AdrienneGiordano.

CPSIA information can be obtained
at www.ICGtesting.com
Printed in the USA
LVHW082233081121
702820LV00014B/765